HOLD THE PRESSES—
THE SWEATHOGS
ARE COMING!

It all started innocently enough. Freddie "Boom-Boom" Washington wrote a story for the school newspaper. It told of the school's brilliant basketball star, a super-cool, super baaad dude who does it all— Freddie "Boom-Boom" Washington. When, for no good reason at all it was rejected, the sweathogs decided to do something about this injustice.

Mr. Kotter made the mistake of telling the sweathogs about freedom of the press, and what started out as a minor issue became a first edition—the beginning of The Sweathog Press. Its motto is: *Give the Readers What They Want. And What They Want is Human Tragedy, Crime and Sex.*

Does it sell? You bet it does. Read all about it in

THE SWEATHOG NEWSHAWKS

So you missed *Welcome Back, Kotter #1*. Well, no hard feelings. You get another chance.

THE SWEATHOG TRAIL, by William Johnston, $1.25 is available now. Ask your local bookseller!

Don't mess it up!

#2

WELCOME BACK, KOTTER

THE SWEATHOG NEWSHAWKS

BY WILLIAM JOHNSTON

tempo
books

Publishers · GROSSET & DUNLAP · New York
A FILMWAYS COMPANY

ONE

Entering the kitchen, Gabe Kotter was holding a tiny tissue paper bandage to his chin.

"Stabbed yourself while shaving?" his wife Julie guessed, pouring coffee for him.

"You should see the other guys," Kotter replied.

Julie looked at him curiously. "Other guys? Are you having your friends in these days to watch you shave?"

"Just a couple old buddies," Kotter replied, sitting down at the table. "Groucho Marx and Jimmy Durante."

"I see." She guessed again. "You were doing imitations in the mirror while you shaved?"

"Right."

"And you got carried away and forgot to watch what you were doing with the razor? And?"

"Groucho lost his mustache and Jimmy Durante now has a pug nose," Kotter told her. He pointed to the two newspapers on the table. "How come?" he asked. "You didn't subscribe to that *other* paper, did you?"

"No," Julie replied, serving breakfast. "That *other* paper belongs to Mr. Bashowitz, down the hall. He's away on vacation, but the boy is still leaving the paper. So, I picked it up. I'm going to save them for him."

"Bashowitz seems like an intelligent guy," Kotter said. "How can he read *that* paper? Look at that headline: 'Bus Bust in Bronx.' And look at that subhead: 'Teen Gang Carries on 20-Block Crime Spree.' "

"So?" Julie asked.

"Is that the most important thing that's happening in the city?" Kotter said. "In *that* paper, crime is the only thing that seems to matter. The world could be coming to an end and they'd feature a candy store holdup in Brooklyn. On the other hand," he said, pointing again, "look at the headline on *my* paper. 'Need For Quality Control in Clothing Industry.' Now, that's something that affects us all. We *all* wear clothes. But how many of us ride the buses in the Bronx?"

"Oh, I don't know . . . I prefer crime for breakfast," Julie said. "It wakes me up."

Grumbling to himself, Kotter read the headline story in the first paper. "This 'teen gang' was actually two kids," he reported. "They got on a bus in the Bronx and rode for twenty blocks without paying."

"It's the same story!" Julie said, looking up from the second paper.

"What's the same story?"

"This story about the clothing industry. It's about the two boys who got on a bus in the Bronx and rode twenty blocks without paying."

"Impossible. What's the connection?"

"According to *your* paper, the boys had holes in their pockets and lost their money, that's why they didn't pay. Your paper feels that the fault lies with the clothing industry, which isn't making pockets the way it used to."

Kotter considered for a moment, then nodded. "That makes a lot of sense."

"How can two newspapers see the same thing so differently?" Julie said.

"Beauty is in the eye of the beholder," Kotter explained. "That also goes for crime and pants pockets. For instance," he said, "do you know how this paper would have covered the story about the little old woman who had so many children that she didn't know what to do? I can see the headline: 'Welfare Mother Exposed as Owner of Luxury Shoe.' "

"And in *your* paper," Julie countered, "the headline would have been: 'Link Seen Between Population Explosion and Sub-Standard Housing.' "

"In *this* paper," Kotter said, "the Muffet story would have been headlined: 'Spider Invasion Threatens Tuffet-Sitters.' "

"In *your* paper, it would have been: 'Significance to Humans Studied in Finding That Spiders Thrive on Diet of Curds and Whey.' "

"That could be important," Kotter said. "Someday, on a steady diet of curds and whey, humans could have as many legs as spiders. One person could ride a bicycle built for two—and have enough legs left over to jog along behind the bicycle at the same time. We could double—triple—the amount of exercise we get. And before long we'd all be as healthy as spiders."

"Speaking of newspapers . . ."

"I thought we were talking about spiders."

"Not any more. Talking about spiders gives me a crawly feeling," Julie said. "Speaking of newspapers, didn't you tell me that Washington was writing a piece for the school newspaper? How did that work out?"

"I don't know. The paper isn't out yet." He frowned thoughtfully. "It comes out today, I think."

"You must really feel good about it," Julie said.

Kotter shook his head. "Nah—it's a lousy paper. I don't care if it ever comes out."

"No, I mean about Washington writing a piece for it. You must have encouraged him to do it."

"Not me. It was his own idea."

"But he must have gotten the incentive from you."

"He got the incentive from the paper," Kotter told her. "The last issue had a story on the basketball team and Washington was only mentioned once. Not only that, his name was misspelled."

"How did they spell it?"

"L-i-n-c-o-l-n."

"A natural mistake."

"So, he decided to write his own story on the team," Kotter said. "He covered the first game."

"Wasn't he playing?"

"Wasn't he playing? He played three positions—forward, coach and sports reporter." Kotter rose. "My congratulations on the breakfast," he said. "Best curds and whey I ever tasted."

"I know what you spiders like," Julie said, rising and following him from the kitchen. "Besides, it's good for your legs."

At the door they kissed.

"Any big plans for today?" Kotter asked.

"No. I'm just going to sit around on my tuffet and wait for you to come home and attack me."

"You Muffet women are all alike," Kotter said, departing.

"Alike how?" Julie called after him teasingly.

"And, besides that, you read the wrong newspaper," Kotter answered.

When Kotter arrived at the school, a student was passing out copies of the school newspaper, the *Booster*, at the door.

"What's the big story?" Kotter asked, accepting a copy.

"The Biology Club's frog stopped croaking," the student replied.

"Lost its voice?"

"No, it croaked."

"One way or another, that was bound to happen to it, hanging around with those cut-ups in the Biology Club," Kotter said, walking on.

In his classroom, Kotter sat down at his desk with the school paper and looked for Washington's story. It was not there. As he was concluding the search, Mr. Piper, the science teacher, entered.

"Sorry about your frog," Kotter said.

"I think it knew it was going to be dissected," Piper said. "It took the easy way out."

"You mean . . ."

"Suicide," Piper said. "I found a tiny vial of poison inside its little cage. That's what happens when you bring a frog into a school. It picks up the language and figures out what's going to happen."

"Too bad the students can't do that," Kotter said.

"Commit suicide?" Piper responded, appalled.

"Pick up the language," Kotter said. He pointed to the school paper. "How come that story says the frog died a natural death?" he asked.

"Mr. Woodman edited out the poison. In any newspaper that Mr. Woodman is in charge of, all deaths are natural. He doesn't want the students to know that there are other ways of dying."

"I can't picture Mr. Woodman being that soft-hearted."

"That's not it. He doesn't want the students to get ideas. He knows he isn't well-liked."

The bell rang.

"I've got to get on the phone and order another frog," Piper said, leaving.

"And hide the poison," Kotter warned.

"That won't do any good. Frogs find ways. The frog before last impaled himself on a ballpoint pen."

A few moments after Piper had gone, the sweathogs began arriving. Washington was muttering angrily and the others looked equally incensed. They dropped heavily into their seats. Washington then got up and strode to Kotter's desk and picked up a book and slammed it down.

"What was that for?" Kotter asked.

"I felt like it," Washington explained.

"Why didn't you use your own book and your own desk?"

"What if I'd ruined the book? What if I'd broke the desk? I'd have to buy a new book and pay for a new desk."

Kotter nodded. "I see the logic."

Washington turned and stomped back to his own desk and sat down heavily again.

"I seem to sense that somebody is unhappy about something," Kotter said. "Could it be something somebody ate? I thought *I* was the only one who had curds and whey for breakfast."

"What's curds and whey, Mr. Kotter?" Horshack asked.

"Spider food."

"You had flies for breakfast?"

"Your wife mad at you again, Mr. Kotter?" Vernajean asked.

"No, it's a new diet," Kotter told her. "One look at a dish of curds and whey and you lose your appetite for food forever."

"Hahh . . . hahh . . . hahh . . ." Horshack hooted.

"About the unhappiness . . ." Kotter said.

"Washington got axed," Barbarino told him.

"Oh? Who asked him to do what?"

"Not asked. Axed. Chopped down."

"How?"

Washington answered. "That story I wrote for the *Booster,*" he said irately. "Mr. Woodman wouldn't let it in. Man, I worked hard on that story. I put in the periods and everything. I even put in some extra periods at the end, so if I left any out in the middle, they could scatter them around where they belonged."

"Did Mr. Woodman say why he rejected the story?" Kotter asked.

"No. All he said was that it was abrobidomenal. But he wouldn't tell me why he wouldn't use it."

"Abrobidomenal?" Kotter asked, baffled.

"Something like that."

Kotter thought for a moment. "Abominable? Is that what he said it was—abominable?"

"Yeah," Washington replied. "What's that mean?"

"Well . . . uh, it means he didn't think much of your story. He didn't say why, though?"

"He didn't *have* to say why," Washington answered. "I *know* why. He couldn't stand to have a good story like mine in with all that junk he puts in that paper. Who wants to read about a dead frog when they can read about a star?"

"Do you still have your story?" Kotter asked.

"Yeah, man. I'm gonna frame it. Barbarino's got a frame that used to have his sister in it. He's gonna give it to me."

"My sister got married," Barbarino explained to Kotter. "I gave her husband the picture for a wedding present."

"Thoughtful," Kotter said. He faced Washington again. "Could we hear the story?" he asked.

"You want me to read it to you?" Washington responded, pleased.

"Yes. Maybe we can figure out why Mr. Woodman rejected it. It might be something minor that can be easily fixed."

Washington got a sheet of paper from between the pages of a book and rose. "You want me to read the periods, too?" he asked Kotter.

"That won't be necessary. Just the words."

Washington stood erect and cleared his throat, then read:

> "Well, folks, here it is the first game of the season. Washington, the star of the

team, is out there on the floor taking prac-
tice shots. The crowd is going wild, crying
'Washington! Washington! Washington!'
But Washington is cool, he don't pay no
attention. Look at how that Washington
handles that ball! There's a hook shot.
The ball goes up perfect and drops
through the hoop without even touching
the net! All the foxes in the stands are
shouting 'Washington! Washington! Washington!' Man, those foxes really get shook
up when they see that Washington shoot
those baskets. But, being the star, Washington is cool about it. Like Washington
once told this reporter, folks, 'I don't even
hear all that cheering and yelling that's
coming from up in the stands, 'cause I
don't want it to spoil my concentration.'
Man, that's cool!

"There's the whistle, folks. Washington
goes over to the bench and calls the coach
and the rest of the team around him and
tells them his strategy. To the rest of the
team, Washington is kind of a god. He
don't like it, he'd rather just be one of the
gang. But I guess it can't be helped if
those other guys on the team and all those
foxes up there in the stands know a god
when they see one. Like Washington once
told this reporter, 'That's the way it is,
man.'

"There's the whistle again, folks! The

game is on! And Washington goes out and wins it!"

Washington, preening, sat down.

"That was an exciting game," Kotter said dryly. "Also, I think, the shortest game on record."

"After the game started, I didn't have any time to watch what was going on," Washington explained.

"All right, class," Kotter said, "can anybody guess why Mr. Woodman turned that story down?"

" 'Cause it's got foxes in it," Vernajean said. "Mr. Woodman don't like foxes and dudes in the same story. He says there's enough of that stuff in the school already, he don't want it in the paper."

Kotter shook his head. "I don't think that was his reason on this one."

"He probably didn't like all the cheering and yelling in the story," Barbarino guessed.

"Yeah, he probably held his hands over his eyes when he read about those cheers," Washington said.

"His hands over his eyes?"

"Like he holds his hands over his ears when he hears yelling in the halls."

"Any other guesses?" Kotter asked.

"He don't like sweathogs, that's the main reason," Epstein said. "Anything we do, he puts it down."

"In this case, though, I suspect there was another reason," Kotter said. "Let me give you a clue." He turned to Washington again. "What were you supposed to be reporting on?" he asked.

"The game."

"But about nine-tenths of your story was about you, and only about one-tenth on the game," Kotter said.

"That makes ten-tenths on the game," Washington said. " 'Cause I *am* the game."

"But you didn't write about what happened during the game," Kotter said. "What you wrote was, if I remember correctly: 'The game is on and Washington goes out and wins it.' "

Washington brightened. "Oh, yeah, now I see what I did wrong," he said.

"Good."

"Mr. Woodman wanted me to say some other dude won the game," Washington said. "He can't stand it, a sweathog winning the game." He shook his head. "I can't do that. I got to tell it like it is. When I win the game, I got to say it."

"No, no," Kotter said. "What I'm telling you is: Your story wasn't a story on a basketball game, it was an advertisement for yourself."

"It was *my* story," Washington replied. "What was it supposed to be an advertisement for—old Woodman? Is that what he wanted?"

"Yeah, you can't get around it, Mr. Kotter," Barbarino said. "The only thing wrong with that story was that Washington wrote it. And Washington is a sweathog. And, to Mr. Woodman, sweathogs are the pits."

Rosalie spoke up. "You want some more proof?" she said to Kotter. "The proof is, I wrote a poem once, and Mr. Woodman wouldn't put *it* in the paper either. He won't put anything in if it don't say what he wants it to say."

"Just read what's on your desk," Epstein said, "*that*'s the proof. Look at those stories in that paper."

Kotter lowered his eyes to the school newspaper and

read aloud the first headline that caught his attention. "'Junior F.B.I. Program Established.' What's that about?"

"You turn in a litterer and you get a pin that says you're a member of the Junior F.B.I.," Barbarino explained. "Mr. Woodman thought it up."

Kotter read another headline. "'Assistant Principal Announces Quiet in the Halls Week.' I can guess what that story is about," he said.

"Yeah, that's right next to the big story on 'Wipe Your Shoes Before You Enter the School Week,'" Washington said.

Kotter turned to the back page and read another headline. "'Students Can Learn From the Animals.' What's that about?"

"That's the movie review," Vernajean said. "He wants us all to go see 'Bambi.'"

"That's not the school newspaper, that's Woodman's newspaper," Epstein said.

"Well," Kotter said, "we live in a free enterprise society, you know."

The sweathogs stared at him blankly.

"One of the advantages of the free enterprise system is that it gives you the opportunity to compete," Kotter explained.

"Hey, yeah—that's right!" Barbarino said. "The next time the school paper comes out, we'll grab all the copies and dump them."

"That isn't quite what I had in mind," Kotter said.

"Yeah, dump them where?" Washington said to Barbarino. "Use your head, man. If we dump them, old Woodman will send out his Junior F.B.I. and find them. We'll get sent up for littering. We got to take them papers down to the school furnace and burn them."

"What I was thinking about was starting your own paper," Kotter said.

There was silence.

"Mr. Kotter, we don't know anything about putting out a newspaper," Horshack said finally. "We don't even have a press. What's the use of yelling 'Stop the presses!' if you don't have a press?"

"You don't need a press," Kotter replied. "The school doesn't have a press either. The school paper is sent out to be printed."

"Who'd put it together, though?" Horshack said. "Somebody has to put it together, don't they, before it goes to the printer?"

"Yeah, if somebody don't put it together, how does the printer know the back page from the front page?" Epstein said.

"I don't think that makes any difference," Barbarino said. "My old man only reads the back page anyway. That's where the sports are. But if the sports was on the front page, he could switch. He's no dummy."

"If we had a paper of our own, we could run old Woodman right out of business," Washington said, warming to the idea. He beamed. "I could be the sports reporter."

"I'll be the poem reporter," Rosalie said. "I think that poem I wrote is still hanging around somewhere."

"I got some great stories," Barbarino said. "Remember that time Moose Regan stuck his cigar in his coat pocket so he could use both hands to turn in a false fire alarm? And when the fire trucks got there, Moose was stomping on his coat and they hit him with a blast from the hose?"

"Everybody's heard that," Epstein said.

"Yeah, but it's a great story," Barbarino insisted.

"Who's gonna write all this stuff?" Washington asked.

"You wrote up the story on the basketball game, didn't you?" Kotter said. "And Rosalie wrote a poem."

"I'm a writer!" Washington said, amazed. "I didn't know that. I knew I was cool, but I didn't know I was *that* cool!"

"What are we going to call the paper?" Vernajean said.

"How about the *Washington Times*?" Washington said. "That makes it sound important."

"It's not going to be printed in Washington," Epstein said.

"Not *that* Washington," Washington said. He pointed to himself. "*This* Washington."

"If we're going to name it after one of us, how about the *Barbarino Bugle*?" Barbarino said.

"Or the *Horshack Hotsheet*," Horshack offered. "Hahh . . . hahh . . . hahh . . ."

"Let's call it the *Sweathog*," Epstein suggested.

A cheer went up.

"I don't know . . ." Kotter said. "The *Sweathog*? A newspaper?"

"Yeah," Washington said. "The *Times* and the *News*—that stuff is too far out."

Kotter blinked at him. "Far out?"

"Far out like those old time groups," Washington explained. "You remember. The Andrews Sisters—that was a group. What kind of a name is that for a group?

A group, man, is called The Velvet Underground or Shanana or The Smago Frenk. We don't want no far out name like The Andrew Sisters or the *Times* or the *News*."

Kotter blinked again. "The *Sweathog* is perfect," he said.

"Man, the *Sweathog* is going to stomp the *Booster* right out of town!" Washington said.

"I got *another* great story," Barbarino said. "Remember the day I put my shoes on the wrong feet and kept running into myself everytime I tried to turn a corner?"

"That was me," Horshack said.

"Oh, yeah . . ." Barbarino said, remembering.

"There's one little thing . . ." Kotter said. "The free enterprise system has some disadvantages, too. One of those disadvantages is that it costs money to start a newspaper."

"Money?" Washington said. "What for? We got the writers, me and Rosalie."

"Printing the paper costs money," Kotter informed him.

"That's okay," Epstein said. "We'll sell the paper. That way, we'll make money."

"But before you can sell a paper, you have to *have* a paper," Kotter pointed out. "And before you can *have* a paper, you have to have it printed. And—pardon me for repeating myself—printing costs money."

"What kind of money are we talking about?" Washington asked.

"This is only a guess . . . a hundred dollars, two hundred?"

"That's the wrong kind of money," Washington said glumly.

"Mr. Kotter," Horshack said, "would you be interested in getting in on the ground floor of a new newspaper with unlimited possibilities for success?"

"I certain would," Kotter replied. "But the *Sweathog* is something else."

As one, the sweathogs sighed dismally.

"I'm sorry. I should have mentioned the part about the money earlier," Kotter said.

"That's okay. You can't think of everything . . . at your age," Barbarino said. "My old man is like that too. He forgets. Last year he forgot to come home for January."

"There's one other thing you could do," Kotter said. "You could try to get on the staff of the school newspaper. Then, maybe you could make some changes."

"What's the chances of Mr. Woodman letting a sweathog get on the staff?" Washington asked.

"Miracles happen," Kotter replied.

"What are the chances of changing Mr. Woodman's mind about what goes in the school paper?" Barbarino asked.

Kotter thought for a second. "Actually, I've never believed in miracles," he said.

The bell rang.

The sweathogs rose and filed out the same way they had arrived, muttering and grumbling.

TWO

"But wouldn't that be super stuff, putting old Woodman out of business with the *Sweathog*?" Washington said to Barbarino as they left the school together that afternoon after classes. "We'd come on strong, see. Headlines about a foot high. Can't you see it? 'Washington Named High School Superstar of the Year!' Man, we could *sell* papers like that. Everybody'd want to read about it."

"Yeah, you'd take a couple hundred copies yourself," Barbarino said.

"It beats reading about a dead frog."

"I don't know ..." Barbarino said. "That was a pretty good story about the frog—until the end. I thought it was going to turn into a dead prince. But it just stayed a frog."

Washington reached out and stopped a girl who was about to move past them. "Hey, I'm taking a survey," he said to her. "If you was gonna buy a paper, which paper would you buy, the one with the story about the dead frog or the one with the story about the high school superstar of the year?"

"I like stories about movie stars," she answered.

"Okay, which has got a better chance of being a movie star, a high school superstar or a frog?"

The girl frowned thoughtfully. "How many guesses do I get?"

Washington released her, sending her on her way. "I'll ask somebody else," he said to Barbarino. "That's the way you do a survey. You keep asking until you get the answer you want."

"Ask all you want," Barbarino said. "It won't help. What we need is money."

They had reached a small printing shop. Washington stopped and peered in through the grimy window.

"We don't have the money, man," Barbarino reminded him again.

"How do we know?" Washington said. "We don't know how much it costs. Let's go in and find out."

Barbarino reached into his pocket and extracted the contents. "If it costs more than three pennies, two bottle caps and about a half-ounce of lint, I'm out," he said.

"What's it gonna hurt?" Washington said, entering the shop.

Barbarino followed him and they found themselves in a small, dark anteroom. From the rear of the shop came the sound of the presses. They moved on, then stopped again at a door that had "Office" painted on it in large, scraggly, uneven letters. Cautiously, Washington opened the door. Inside, a gray-haired man with a full, droopy mustache was seated at a rolltop desk. He was counting money, piling bills in stacks of fives, tens and twenties.

Sighting Washington and Barbarino, the man leaped to his feet and threw up his hands. "Take my life—don't touch the cash!" he said fearfully.

"Cool it, man," Washington said. "This isn't any stickup."

The man lowered his arms. "In this neighborhood, that's the first thing I think of, a stickup," he said. "Everybody that comes in, I put up my hands. Better safe than sorry. Besides, it's the only exercise I get." He looked at Washington and Barbarino closely. "If you're not here to stick me up, what do you want?"

"We're here on business, kind of," Washington told him.

The man smiled broadly. "You came to the right place," he said, extending a hand. "Happy Harrison is the name, and business is the game."

Barbarino and Washington shook hands with him.

Happy Harrison pointed to the water cooler. "You want a drink first, or shall we get right down to the details?" he said.

"There's no water in that thing," Barbarino said.

"Good. Saves time. Now, what can I do for you? A phony high school diploma? Something a little more classy—maybe a college degree? I got a Medical Doctor degree all made up that I can let you have for a price. The guy who ordered it cut his finger on a beer can on the way to pick it up and went out of his head at the sight of blood."

"No, what we're thinking about, see, is starting up a newspaper," Washington said.

"Aha! Brilliant!" Happy Harrison said. "It's what

the world needs—another newspaper. Is it a daily? A weekly?"

"It's kind of a whenever-we-get-enough-stuff-to-put-in-it," Barbarino told him.

"That's the best kind. I make a bigger profit on every-once-in-awhile business," Harrison said. "When do we go to press, as you newspaper boys say?"

"What about the cost?" Washington asked.

"The cost? Is that important? Newspapering is an honored profession. Who cares about the money?" He looked at them closely again. "What would you guess—about the cost?"

"Would it be more than three pennies, two bottle caps and a half-ounce of lint?" Barbarino asked.

Happy Harrison's eyes narrowed. "That's what you got to spend?"

"About. The lint might go to a full ounce."

"Gentlemen, you are out of the newspaper business," Happy Harrison informed them.

"We haven't been in it yet," Washington said. "We're *thinking* about it, see. That's why we're talking money."

"First, the money. Then, the talk," Harrison said. He motioned toward the door. "Go get your money together, then come back."

"We haven't got any money to get together," Washington said. "But, what I was thinking was . . ."

Happy Harrison interrupted. "When I said your money, I didn't mean *your* money," he said, "I meant your *money*."

Washington and Barbarino peered at him puzzledly.

"Only a fool starts a business on his *own* money," Harrison told them. "You use somebody else's money.

When I started this print shop, did I use my own money? What am I, a fool? I used the bank's money."

"I don't think any bank is going to give us any money," Barbarino said.

"Yeah, the only way a bank would give *us* any money would be under conditions where, later on, a judge would give us twenty years."

"You don't need a bank," Happy Harrison said. "You got something to trade for money. You got a newspaper. A newspaper has space in it. You can trade that space to people who want to advertise."

"Hey, yeah—sell advertising!" Washington said.

"And with the money you get for advertising, you can pay your printer," Harrison said. "What is left over, that's the profit." He chuckled. "That's a little humor—about the profit."

Washington headed for the door. "Let's go!" he said to Barbarino. "We got selling to do!"

When they left the print shop they began looking for Epstein and Horshack. They found them a short time later and told them about the plan to finance the newspaper with advertising. Epstein was enthusiastic. He immediately named himself the advertising manager of the paper. But the idea saddened Horshack.

"I can't sell anything," Horshack said. "I can't even give anything away. I have to pay people to take things from me. And I can't afford to pay people to buy advertising."

"Just watch me, man, I'll show you how to do it," Washington said.

They chose the nearby supermarket to be their first advertiser. When they entered the store they found the manager building a display with large cans of tomatoes.

"Excuse me, sir . . ." Washington began.

"No," the manager said.

"You see, me and my friends—"

"No."

"—we are starting a newspaper. This paper is going to be the—"

"No!" the manager said again, continuing to stack cans.

"—the greatest," Washington went on. "This is going to be the kind of paper that is sold out before it even gets off the presses."

"No!" the manager said. He motioned to Horshack, who, in his eagerness to learn how to sell, was edging close to the rising pyramid of cans. "Back!" he barked.

"Naturally," Washington continued, "the advertisers are going to be fighting to get into this paper with their ads."

"No, no and no."

"So, now is the time to buy in and avoid the rush," Washington told him.

"No."

"Right now, we can let you have a full page," Washington said. "Later, you'll probably be lucky to get a square inch. And a newspaper space is just like a can of coffee. When it's hard to get, the price goes up."

"No."

"You're gonna be sorry when all the other supermarkets take out ads and steal all your customers," Washington warned.

"This is the only supermarket in the neighborhood."

"Let me put it another way . . ." Washington began again.

At that moment, Horshack, who had edged close

once more, bumped the stack of cans. The top two tiers toppled, setting off a can-slide. The entire pyramid crashed, sending cans rolling in all directions.

The manager stiffened, staring.

A can from the first stack rolled into the base of a second stack a short distance away. The second stack began to crumble, then, suddenly, with a loud crash, collapsed, shooting more cans across the floor.

The manager faced the sweathogs. There was fear in his eyes.

Another pyramid collapsed. Then another and another. The entire floor appeared to be carpeted with cans.

"I understand," the manager said shakily to Washington. "Yes! Yes, I'll take an ad. I'll take a full page. Is that what you want—a full page?"

Washington and the other sweathogs, surprised by his reaction to the damage that Horshack had done, stared at him in wonder.

"One full page and one square inch!" the manager said.

"Sold . . ." Washington replied feebly.

The manager pulled a roll of bills from his pocket, peeled a number of the bills from it, then shoved them into Washington's hand. "Is that enough?"

"Yeah, that's . . ."

"Then, please!" the manager said, making shooing motions.

Still in a state of bafflement, the sweathogs left the store.

"Man, I must really be a salesman!" Washington said when they got outside. "I sold that guy an ad even though Horshack almost wrecked his store."

"You know what I think?" Epstein said. "Did you see the look in that guy's eyes? He was scared. He wasn't buying advertising. He was buying protection."

"From what?" Barbarino asked.

"From us. He thought if he didn't buy that ad we'd come back and wreck his store again."

"You mean *I* sold that ad!" Horshack said, elated. "A first!"

Washington thought for a moment, studying Horshack. Then he said, "And what you can do once, you can do again."

Horshack looked dismayed. "You want me to go back to that supermarket and knock over more cans?"

"Not the supermarket! Another store," Washington told him. He looked up the street. "That drugstore," he said, pointing.

"Isn't this the old protection racket?" Barbarino said, as the sweathogs walked on toward the drugstore.

"Never heard of it," Washington replied. "All I know is, if you knock something over, somebody buys an ad. That's good enough for me."

They entered the drugstore, McNary's Pharmacy. The elderly man behind the counter watched them warily as they approached.

"Mr. McNary?" Washington said.

"Who's asking?" the man replied.

"You see before you the brains of this neighborhood's new newspaper," Washington told him.

"I don't carry no pornography," McNary said.

"No, this is a *news*paper. It's got news in it," Washington told him. "It's called the *Sweathog* and it's the greatest." He nudged Horshack. "Go to work."

Horshack sauntered toward a nearby display.

"We are here to give you the opportunity of a lifetime," Washington said to McNary. "If you act fast, you can get a page of advertising in the *Sweathog* before the prices go up."

There was a crash, as the display hit the floor.

"Oh-oh—clumsy me," Horshack said.

"Oh-oh, clumsy you, pick that stuff up!" McNary ordered.

"Wait a minute!" Washington said. "That was an accident. That's the kind of accident that can happen. You understand? Accidents like that can happen *all the time*."

"If it happens in here again," McNary said, "I'll have the whole crowd of you in the cooler for vandalism!"

"I guess we better go back to the supermarket," Horshack said dismally, beginning the chore of picking up the items from the display.

McNary faced Washington again. "If I buy some advertising in this newspaper, what's in it for me?" he asked.

"Customers, man!"

"What about my competitor up the street, Finnery's Pharmacy, is he advertising?"

"Not yet. But if you want to buy all the space in the paper and keep him out, we're ready to listen to a deal."

"Tell you what I'll do," McNary said. "I'll buy an ad and you give me a story."

"Done!" Washington said. "What kind of a story do you want? How about a story on a fire? Or a big drug bust?"

"No, no, a story on my store," McNary said. "A

story that tells what a fine store I got, with the lowest prices and the best service—better than that low-down double-dealer up the street, Finnery. A true story of facts, that's all I want."

"That'd cost you a little more," Washington said. "Writing a story is extra."

"I'll write it myself, when I write the ad," McNary said. "What's so hard about it? It's the same thing, the ad and the story."

"You got a deal," Washington said. "One ad and one story, same price."

The sweathogs collected for the advertisement, then left the drugstore.

"We got it made!" Washington said when they were outside. "All we got to do is give away a story with every advertisement."

"How come I never see any stories like that in regular papers?" Barbarino said.

"They never thought of it," Washington replied. "They'd be full of stories on stores if they knew they could sell advertising like that. You just watch, once they see what we're doing, they'll all start." He motioned. "Come on! Let's hit Finnery with what McNary's doing. Finnery'll want an ad and a story too."

The late TV movie was just beginning. Kotter and Julie were seated on the couch in front of the set, sharing a large bowl of popcorn.

"This is a classic," Kotter said.

"It is for us," Julie said. "We've seen it twelve times."

"You're exaggerating. Six at the most."

"I still don't know what it's about," Julie said. "Just

when I finish reading the subtitle, the scene changes. The hero is saying something like 'Your lips are like dew-wet cherries,' and I see a load of wet laundry hanging on a line."

"You ought to take a speed reading course," Kotter said.

The doorbell rang.

"Who could that be?" Julie said.

"It's not opportunity," Kotter replied, rising. "Opportunity knocks."

Kotter opened the door, and the sweathogs, accompanied by Rosalie and Vernajean, swarmed into the apartment.

"We did it!" Washington announced triumphantly. "We got a newspaper!"

"Big deal," Kotter said, closing the door. "I've got two newspapers in the kitchen. One of them belongs to a neighbor."

"I mean we got a newspaper of our own—the *Sweathog!*" Washington said. "We got a printer to print it and we got advertising to pay for it!"

"That's wonderful!" Julie said from the couch.

"Is this for real?" Kotter said doubtfully.

"We been working on it since school let out," Barbarino told him. "We got a real printer to print it. And we got advertising—from the supermarket and from two drugstores and a restaurant and a guy that sells TV sets off the back of a truck and a lot of others."

"Miracles *do* happen," Kotter said, amazed.

"All we got to do now," Horshack said, "is get some more stories and put the paper together for the printer."

"*More* stories?" Kotter said. "What stories do you already have?"

"Well, there's my report on the basketball game," Washington said, "and Rosalie's poem ... and then some other stuff ..."

"Also," Epstein said, "we need an office."

"Yeah, you can't have a newspaper without a newspaper office," Washington said.

Kotter nodded. "Makes sense."

"It doesn't have to be a big office," Vernajean said. "It can be a little office. Like ... oh ..." She looked around. "Like ... oh ... about the size of this room ..."

"You all live in apartments," Kotter said. "One of those apartments must have a room about the size of this room."

"We can't use my place," Vernajean said. "My mother don't like noise."

"Yeah, and my old man says we can't use our place either," Washington said. "He says he sees too much of us as it is."

"And my old lady says why don't we set up our office on the street, that's where we spend all our time anyway," Barbarino said.

"Why don't you move in with the printer?" Kotter suggested.

"We thought of that," Washington replied. "But he wants to charge us rent. And we just made enough on the advertising to pay for the printing."

"What we were thinking ..." Vernajean said, looking around again.

"I *know* what you're thinking," Kotter said. "And

the answer is no. This is my home, it's not a newspaper office."

"We'd give you a free ad in the paper," Barbarino said.

"What would I advertise?"

"You could sell some of this furniture," Horshack said. "It's a little crowded in here for an office."

"No!"

"Shall I knock over his stack of cans?" Horshack asked Washington.

Washington ignored the question. "It won't be for long," he said to Kotter. "Just until we make enough money to buy our own building, like regular papers."

"No!"

"Honey," Julie said to Kotter, "it might be fun."

Kotter headed for the kitchen. "We'll discuss it in private," he said.

Julie got up and hurried after him.

"Don't worry about your popcorn while you're gone," Barbarino called after them. "I'll watch it."

In the kitchen, Kotter and Julie squared off.

"I like them," Kotter said, "but I don't want to live with them. Not *all* of them all at once."

"Gabe, it would probably be for only a few minutes a day. And it would be exciting, don't you think? I mean, a newspaper. Right here in our own apartment. You know how newspapers are, the hustle and bustle."

"This is our *home*!"

"Big stories!" Julie said. "Everything that happens, we'd be the first to know."

"When I come home at night, I want to come home to *you*—not sweathogs."

"Gabe, according to what you told me, you encouraged them to start this paper. You have a responsibility. If they don't have an office, how can they run a newspaper?"

"Do you realize that already our popcorn is gone?" Kotter said. "That's what would happen to all of the food in the house every day—gone!"

"But, didn't you see how excited they are about this newspaper? They're really *interested* in something. Isn't it worth giving up a little of our privacy to encourage that?"

"I'll tell you what they're interested in. They want to run the school newspaper out of business."

"Well, isn't that what all businessmen want? To ruin their competitors?"

Kotter sighed. "I guess I did get them started on this," he said.

"And the newspaper *might* be a success," Julie said. "I mean, someday there might be a plaque up in this apartment, saying here is where it all started."

"What the plaque will say is 'Here is where Gabe Kotter went out of his mind.' "

"Honey, can't we at least *try* it?"

"Well ... I guess I *do* have sort of a responsibility ..."

"It's settled!" Julie called out to the sweathogs, leaving the kitchen. "You have your office!"

From the living room came a cheer.

Returning, Kotter went straight to the popcorn bowl. It was empty.

"I thought you were going to watch it," he said to Barbarino.

"I did—until it disappeared."

"All right, all right," Kotter said, addressing the

sweathogs, "you can have your office here. But, there are certain rules. Is that understood?"

"What are the rules, Mr. Kotter?" Horshack asked.

"I'll make them up as we go along."

"Hahh . . . hahh . . . hahh . . ."

"We got work to do, we got stories to write," Washington said to the others. "Let's get at it."

"I got a story," Barbarino said. "Anybody got a pencil?"

"And paper," Washington said. "Mr. Kotter, where's the paper."

"Rule One: you supply your own paper," Kotter said.

"But I have some I can loan you until you get your own," Julie said, setting out for the kitchen again.

"And pencils!" Epstein called after her.

"If this stuff is going to a printer, it ought to be typewritten," Kotter said. "Can anybody type?"

"Somebody can, I guess—all the typewriters they make—but none of us," Rosalie replied.

"I can type," Vernajean said. She held up an index finger. "This is what I do it with."

"Mr. Kotter, you got a typewriter, haven't you?" Washington said.

"I brought that too," Julie said, returning from the kitchen with the typewriter in addition to the paper.

Kotter groaned and returned to the couch. A few moments later, Julie joined him.

"What kind of newspaper office would it have been without a typewriter?" she whispered.

"Watch the movie," Kotter replied testily.

Behind them, the sweathogs began work on the first edition.

"This story is really news," Barbarino said. "I heard it this morning. Remember that guy that lived downstairs from me and moved to the suburbs?"

"That guy that was always breathing all the time?" Washington said.

"Yeah. He's in the hospital. That fresh air in the suburbs got in his lungs and broke up all that stuff that was holding them together, all that corroded gas fumes and the smell from Obermeir's Welding Shop. His lungs went flat."

"That's a *good* story," Washington said. "It's got civic pride. Maybe we can get Obermeirs to take an ad to go with it."

On the couch, Kotter smiled.

"Getting used to having the office in the apartment?" Julie whispered.

"No. That was an expression of relief. I have the feeling that the first edition of the *Sweathog* will also be the last."

THREE

Arriving in the kitchen a few mornings later, Kotter found Julie placing a cup of hot water at his place at the table. Otherwise, the table was bare.

"Am I on a fast?" he asked puzzledly.

"Temporarily," she replied. "The sweathogs worked late last night getting the paper ready for the printer and they snacked while they worked. Water is all we have left."

Kotter opened the door to the cupboard and looked in. "Remember that movie, 'The Giant Cockroach That Ate Philadephia?' " he said. "It wasn't fiction, it was real. The Giant Cockroach passed through Brooklyn last night."

"They were anxious," Julie said. "It's their first issue. When people are anxious, they nibble."

"I'm surprised we still have walls."

"But we don't have that wax fruit we got from one of your relatives one Christmas any more," Julie said.

"Every cloud *does* have its silver lining," Kotter said. He looked at the cup of hot water. "It looks fattening," he said. "I'll stop on the way to school and get something with fewer calories. A chocolate cream doughnut, maybe."

"Just don't say anything to the sweathogs about eating all our food," Julie said. "They didn't realize what they were doing. That paper was the only thing they could think about." She frowned worriedly. "I hope it's a success. They worked so hard on it."

"Hard work is overrated," Kotter said, leaving the kitchen. "It helps more to have talent—or at least a vague idea of what you're doing. From what I overheard last night while the sweathogs were putting their paper to bed, I advise you to expect the worst."

"You've been against this right from the beginning," Julie charged as they reached the door.

"Because their reason for putting out the paper is wrong," Kotter said. "All they want to do is get back at Mr. Woodman for not using Washington's report on the basketball game in the school paper."

"That's not true!"

"What's the other reason?"

"Well . . . they also want to get back at him for not using Rosalie's poem in the school paper."

Kotter kissed her. "I rest my case."

When Kotter reached the school, Horshack was at the main entrance, hawking copies of the *Sweathog*. He had a bundle of the papers under one arm and was waving a copy wildly and crying, "Extra! Extra!" The students, however, were resisting his sales pitch, moving past him without buying.

"What's so extra?" Kotter asked Horshack.

"I've only sold two copies," he replied. He indicated the bundle of papers under his arm. "These are all extra."

"Sales aren't going so well?"

"I've got a bad corner," Horshack said.

"A bad corner? You're at the main door."

"Then maybe it's me," Horshack said. "Look at this face, Mr. Kotter. Would you buy a newspaper from this face?"

"Yes," Kotter replied, handing him a coin and receiving a copy of the *Sweathog*. "Who else bought copies from you?" he asked.

"The student editor of the school paper, for one. And it was a dirty trick."

"How so?"

"He let everybody else read his copy," Horshack explained. "Then the ones who'd read it starting telling the ones who hadn't about it. After that, sales dropped off."

"Who was the other buyer?"

"Mr. Woodman."

"Did he say anything about the paper?" Kotter asked.

Horshack shook his head. "He didn't buy it to read it," he said. "As soon as I gave it to him, he jammed it into the trash basket."

"In itself that was a comment, I suspect," Kotter said. He moved on. "Keep selling!" he called back to Horshack.

Horshack began his cry again. "Extra! Extra!"

In his classroom, Kotter sat down at his desk with the paper. As he read, he continually shook his head in dismay. After a while his eyes began to glaze over. As he was finishing the last page, the bell rang. Kotter closed the paper and leaned back in his chair to await the arrival of the sweathogs.

They came in looking as if they were marchers in a funeral procession. Each sweathog was carrying a large bundle of unsold papers. They dumped the bundles on the floor near the doorway, then slogged on to their seats. Except for an occasional gutteral mutter the room was silent.

"Well, maybe it's the recession," Kotter said sympathetically. "People aren't investing in newspapers the way they used to."

"Six copies," Washington said glumly. "We sold six copies."

"It's a plot," Barbarino said. "The six that bought the paper told everybody else it was lousy."

"Word-of-mouth like that can dry up sales," Kotter said.

"It was bad luck," Epstein said. "Those six that bought just don't know a masterpiece when they read it."

"You don't think it's possible that maybe the paper is lousy?" Kotter said.

"No, man!" Washington replied. "It's a *great* paper!"

"Let's examine that," Kotter said, picking up the copy he had purchased from Horshack. "First—the lead-off story—we have Washington's report on a basketball game that was played almost two weeks ago. Of course, it isn't actually a report on the game. It's a love letter to Washington—by Washington. But, that aside, it's not *news*. It's past history."

"Who says it's got to be new news?" Washington countered. "What's the matter with a little old news? Don't you know there's a nostalgia craze going on?"

"All right, let's take up the second item, Rosalie's poem," Kotter said. He turned to the poem in the paper and read aloud:

> Sometimes when I get blue
> And don't know what to do,
> When things get unbearable,
> Or even worse—terrible—
> And I don't want to talk,
> Or even go for a long walk,
> I just make believe I'm

Kotter lowered the paper. "That's it," he said.

"My baby brother got hold of the poem and tore it," Rosalie explained. "That's all that was left. He ate the ending."

"Couldn't you *remember* the ending?"

She shook her head. "It wasn't a poem about me," she said. "It was a poem about some person that when she gets blue she don't know what to do."

"Rosalie knows what to do," Vernajean said.

"I cover my head with a pillow," Rosalie said.

Kotter returned his attention to the paper. "Moving on," he said, "we have this inspirational piece on McNary's Pharmacy." Again, he read aloud:

> McNary's Pharmacy is the place, not like
> that gyp joint up the street, to get the best
> bargains, with the best selection of clean-
> minded paperback books on the side. Mr.

McNary, who is not in the business to make money but because he wants to serve humanity, is a registered pharmacist of the highest repute and lowest prices. Last year at the Pharmacy Convention, Mr. McNary won the Green Thumb Award for filling prescriptions—an award that the other so-called pharmacist on the block couldn't win if he went to the convention with his thumb already painted green. . . .

Kotter faced the class again. "There's a lot more to the saga of the Green Thumb award, of course—as you well know—but that's an ample sample."

"That's *big* news," Washington said. "Nobody knew about that award till they read it in the *Sweathog*."

"It's interesting that the story is right next to the ad for McNary's Pharmacy," Kotter said.

"It's probably a coincidence, Mr. Kotter," Horshack said.

"And, I suppose, it's also a coincidence that the story on The Dead End Bar & Grill is next to the ad for The Dead End Bar & Grill. And that the story on the Zinser-Hoffman Bagel Shop just happened to be next to the ad for the Zinser-Hoffman Bagel shop. And so on and so on."

"Coincidences are like birds of a feather, Mr. Kotter, they flock together," Horshack said.

"Uh-huh." Kotter turned to the back page of the paper. "I admit, though, I *did* find your movie review very interesting," he said to Horshack.

"You liked it, huh?"

"I didn't say that. I said I found it interesting." He read aloud again:

> What I didn't like about this movie was I got gum on my left shoe. The popcorn was good, but a little salty. Along about the middle, Barbarino came in and sat down across the aisle. I yelled over to him quietly Hey, Vinnie. And he yelled back at me, Hey who's that yelling quietly Hey Vinnie? I said it's me. Then everybody started yelling shut up. So I went over and sat with Barbarino. He thought the popcorn didn't have enough salt on it.

Kotter raised his eyes from the paper. "One thing—you forgot to mention the name of the movie," he told Horshack.

"Another coincidence, Mr. Kotter."

"Coincidence?"

"Yeah, I also forgot to mention where it's playing. Hahh . . . hahh . . . hahh . . ."

Kotter closed the paper. "Is it any wonder that you couldn't sell this thing?" he said. "It's a movie review that doesn't name the movie, and one unfinished poem, and Washington's love letter, and the rest is story after story—all dull—on your advertisers. Who wants to read that?"

"It's our first paper," Washington said. "We were bound to make a couple little mistakes. Don't forget, Mr. Kotter, I'm not putting that paper out alone, so you can't expect it to be perfect."

"I *like* the paper," Barbarino told Kotter. "Look at all them columns, lined up neat."

"Yeah, and those are good stories," Epstein said. "Did you read that story on The Dead End Bar & Grill? Did you know before you read the paper that if your wife calls up there for you they'll tell her she called a wrong number? That's vital information."

"I'd rather read about that than a dead frog," Barbarino said.

"Yeah, Mr. Kotter, we got a *good* paper," Washington insisted. "It's the newspaper *buyers* that went wrong."

The classroom door opened and Mr. Woodman, the assistant principal, came chugging in, beaming.

Kotter and the sweathogs stared at him in disbelief. They had never seen him smiling before.

"Congratulations!" Woodman said. "I've read your newspaper! It's . . . It's . . . Words fail me!"

"That was my reaction," Kotter said.

"Mr. Woodman, how could you read it?" Horshack asked. "You threw it in the trash can."

"That was a mistake," Woodman replied. "I thought I was throwing away the lunch that I bring to work with me every day. When I got to my office and found out I still had my lunch, I rushed right back to the litter basket and retrieved the paper—and discarded the lunch."

"And you liked the *Sweathog?*" Kotter said, looking at Woodman suspiciously.

" 'A' for Effort!" Woodman responded. "I thought it was . . . Well, I thought it was . . . Words still fail me."

"Have you by any chance heard that with the rest of

the readers in the school the paper was a flop?" Kotter asked him.

"Yes, I believe I did hear something like that," Woodman admitted. He addressed the sweathogs again. "But don't let that discourage you. You have a fine paper. Don't change it. The readers just aren't ready for a quality newspaper like the *Sweathog*. But they'll come around. Just keep doing exactly what you're doing now." He turned to Kotter again. "Keep up the good work, Kotter!" Then he departed in the same way that he had arrived, chugging.

Once more, the room was silent.

"Do I hear thinking?" Kotter asked.

"Yeah, you're right, Mr. Kotter, we blew it," Washington said. "If Mr. Woodman likes that paper, it must really be the pits."

"It's like expecting the Nobel Prize and getting the Green Thumb award," Horshack said.

"What's the Nobel Prize?" Barbarino asked.

"It's something Paul Newman got in a movie," Horshack replied.

"You understand, of course, why Mr. Woodman doesn't want you to change the *Sweathog* in any way," Kotter said.

"Because with the *Sweathog* the way it is, the *Booster* has got a clear field," Washington said.

Kotter nodded agreement. "Well, at least you got something out of the experience," he said. "You learned how not to put out a newspaper."

"I got more out of it than the others," Horshack said. "I got gum on my left shoe."

"Hold it!" Washington said. "We're not done! The

Sweathog lives! All we got to do is change it, that's all. Now, we know what to do!"

"What?" Epstein asked.

"We got to do what we didn't do before," Washington said. "If Mr. Woodman likes the paper the way it is, we got to turn it around and make it something else."

"What?" Epstein asked again.

"Easy, man. What we *did* do the last time, we *don't* do this time. That's the way you do the opposite, you do what you didn't—or, if it's the other way around, you don't do what you did."

"What?" Epstein asked once more.

Washington threw up his hands. "I don't know," he said. "Mr. Kotter," he asked, "what do we do?"

Kotter reached into his wastebasket and retrieved a copy of a city newspaper that he had deposited there the day before. "I brought this from home," he said, straightening. "It isn't the newspaper *I* read—I want to make that perfectly clear. It's the newspaper one of my neighbors reads."

"What'd you do, Mr. Kotter," Horshack asked, "beat him to his own paper? Hahh . . . hahh . . . hahh . . ."

"He left it to us when he went away on vacation," Kotter replied, rising. "It's one of the most successful newspapers in the country." He handed the paper to Barbarino. "Look through it. You might learn something about putting out a newspaper that people will buy."

Barbarino opened the paper. "It looks like the *Sweathog*," he said, "a lot of words all lined up in columns."

"It's the formula that counts," Kotter said. "Read some of the words. Maybe you'll get the idea."

"Here's a human tragedy story," Barbarino said. "It's about a guy who lost his Superman Comics collection in a fire."

"There's a crime story," Epstein said, looking over Barbarino's shoulder. "A couple guys got five years for running a protection racket."

"So far," Horshack said, "that's human tragedy and crime. Turn the page."

"Sex," Epstein said.

"It's a story about the birds and the bees," Barbarino reported.

"Vinnie, we know what sex is, you don't have to call it the birds and the bees," Washington said.

"No, this is a sex story about a bird and a bee. At the zoo they crossed a bee and a parrot. It talks to itself. It says, 'Hey, honey, lets buzz on up to my hive.' "

"Is that really what people want, Mr. Kotter?" Vernajean asked.

"People buy this paper," he answered. "They didn't buy your paper."

"Then this is what we do," Washington said. "We give them what they want. We give them human tragedy, sex and crime. We wipe out the *Booster* with one issue!"

"Where do we get stories like that?" Barbarino asked.

Epstein held up the paper that Kotter had passed along to Barbarino. "We get them out of here," he said.

"No, that isn't news any more," Kotter said. "You have to get your own stories—fresh stories."

"Easy," Washington said. "That stuff is all around us—tragedy, sex, crime—right here in the neighborhood. After school," he told the sweathogs, "we fan out. We ask questions. Anything we get on tragedy, sex or crime, it's a story."

"I'll cover sex," Horshack said. "I haven't been to the zoo in a long time."

"Do you want that last chicken leg?" Julie asked Kotter, as they were finishing dinner in the kitchen that evening.

Kotter, distracted, was listening to the sounds of Vernajean's voice and the clicking of the typewriter coming from the living room. "What?" he responded.

"I said do you want that last chicken leg?"

"You can have it."

"No, you take it if you want it."

"Are you sure *you* don't want it?" Kotter said.

"Not if you want it."

"That's okay, you take it."

"Gabe, I don't want it if you want it."

The sound of the typewriter had stopped.

"What's that!" Kotter said nervously.

"What's what?"

"Washington stopped typing."

"Maybe . . ."

Washington appeared in the kitchen. "Man, that is work!" he said exhaustedly. "They built that typewriter crazy. The letters are all scrambled up. First I hunt, then I peck, then I hunt, then I peck." He picked up the chicken leg from the platter. "I ought to be in the typewriter building business," he said, departing. "I don't know how the alphabet goes either."

"The chicken leg is yours," Kotter said to Julie. "All you have to do is wrestle Washington for it."

The doorbell rang.

"I'll get it," Kotter said, rising. "If we're lucky, there's an ordinance against operating a newspaper in an apartment and that's the cops to close us down."

"Gabe, try to think of this as fun!" Julie said.

"Whee!" he said unenthusiastically, departing.

In the living room, Vernajean was on the phone, taking a story from a reporter in the field—Horshack, Barbarino or Epstein.

"Uh-huh, two legs, both broke," she said into the phone, taking notes. "Wow! Broke clean off!"

Kotter winced, then opened the door. Charley Piper was there.

"I tried to call you," Piper said, entering. "But your phone has been busy all evening."

Closing the door, Kotter pointed to Vernajean. "That's the city desk," he said. He then indicated Washington, who was pecking away on the typewriter. "That's rewrite."

Vernajean hung up the phone.

"Who broke both legs, clean off?" Kotter asked her.

"Not a who, Mr. Kotter. It was an it. Horshack was going by a restaurant and looking in and he saw a table collapse when the waiter put the food on it. Two of the table legs broke—clean off."

"And the food spilled on the diners?"

Vernajean nodded.

"A human tragedy story, obviously," Kotter said.

"No, sex," Vernajean told him. "Horshack

recognized the man and woman at the table. They're both married. But they're married to other people."

The phone rang and she picked it up and began taking notes on another story.

"This is exciting!" Piper said. "It's like a real newspaper office."

Julie came in from the kitchen with a tray that held cokes and cookies. She greeted Charley Piper, then supplied Washington with a coke and cookies.

"Oh, my!" Julie said, looking over Washington's shoulder at what he was writing. "Does Gabe know about that?"

"He will when he reads it in the *Sweathog*," Washington replied.

"What's that?" Kotter asked, as Julie moved on, taking a coke and cookies to Vernajean.

"Corruption in the school administration," she told him.

"What? What?" Kotter asked.

"Paper clips are mysteriously disappearing from the supply closet," Julie replied. "The *Sweathog* asks if there's a connection between that and the fact that a certain administrator leaves the school every day with a briefcase."

"Which administrator? Who? Who?"

"A 'bigwig,' " she told him.

"That could be anybody," Kotter said. "Everybody in administration carries a briefcase. It identifies them. It's the only way we have of telling the administrators from the custodians."

Julie shrugged. "All I know is what I read in the paper."

"Stop the typewriter!" Vernajean suddenly called out to Washington.

"Big story!" he asked.

"A fire!" she told him.

"Where is it?"

"It hasn't started yet," Vernajean answered. "But when it does it'll be in the phone booth next to the phone booth from where Epstein is calling from."

"How does Epstein know a fire is going to start?" Kotter asked.

"Because Moose Regan is in the other booth, calling in a false alarm, and he just dropped his cigar in his coat pocket," Vernajean told him. She turned to Washington again. "Start the typewriter!" she said. "Epstein smells smoke!"

Washington began pecking away.

"Flames!" Vernajean reported. "Moose is running out of the phone booth! He's rolling around on the sidewalk! Here comes the fire engines!"

"Not so fast!" Washington complained.

Vernajean spoke into the phone. "Hold the fire engines!" She listened for a moment, then turned to Washington again. "Too late," she said. "The firemen have got the hoses on Moose already." She listened again. "Moose is up and running. The firemen are chasing him with the hose!" she reported. "Oh-oh."

"What happened?" Kotter asked.

"They all disappeared down into the subway," Vernajean said. She hung up. "Did you get that?" she asked Washington.

"Give me time," he replied crossly, still pecking away.

"What have you got so far?"

" 'Epstein smells smo—' "

The phone rang again. Vernajean picked it up, listened, then called out to Washington again. "Stop the typewriter!"

"What now?" he asked.

"The volcano's erupting!" she reported.

"Wait a minute!" Kotter said. "What volcano? This is Brooklyn!"

"Some people call it the garbage dump," Vernajean said. "But Horshack says when it's on fire and the chicken fat is melting and running down the sides it looks like a volcano."

"How many 'k's in volcano?" Washington asked, with a finger poised over a typewriter key.

FOUR

"This is the day! The second edition of the *Sweathog* comes out!" Julie said excitedly as Kotter entered the kitchen for breakfast. "How can you look so calm?"

"A man who has lived through the eruption of a chicken fat volcano can face anything," he replied, sitting down at the table.

"But this is a kind of test for the sweathogs," she said. "Remember how down they were when the first edition of their paper flopped? This will show if they can come back after being cast down into the pits!"

Kotter looked at her levelly. "I think you've got a plot for a TV movie there," he said. "How was that again?"

"Flop. Pits. Test."

"Then don't worry about it," Kotter said. "If it's a test, the sweathogs have the answers written down on little scraps of paper, which they'll come upon at the right moment." He poured cereal into a bowl. "Here's one of the answers now," he said, as a folded piece of paper dropped out of the box.

"What does it say?"

Kotter unfolded the piece of paper and read. "With fruit, milk or cream and sugar, a bowl of this cereal will provide the same nourishment as fruit, milk or cream and sugar." He looked at Julie. "I wonder what the question was?"

"The question is: Will the *Sweathog* be a flop or a hit?"

"I have a better question: Where is the fruit for the cereal?"

"Oh ... I don't think there is any," Julie said, going to the refrigerator. "The sweathogs worked late last night, remember. I'm surprised that there's even cereal." She opened the refrigerator. "Honestly, don't you think the paper has a good chance this time? From what I overheard, it seems to have everything they decided it should have, human tragedy, crime and sex. No fruit," she reported.

"That's all right. How many people buy a paper to read about fruit anyway."

"I mean no fruit for your cereal," she said, going to the cupboard.

"The only exception to that that I can remember is the Great Banana Rebellion of 1840," Kotter said. "It was a protest against those jokes about people slipping on banana skins. Bananas refused to give up their skins until the jokes were banned."

"Here's a raisin," Julie said, emerging from the cupboard.

"*One* raisin?"

"The sweathogs missed it, I guess. It must have dropped out of the box. I found it on the shelf." She dropped it into his cereal bowl, splashing milk. "Sorry," she said. "It was heavier than I thought."

"Raisins have iron," Kotter said.

"How did the Great Banana Rebellion end?"

"Oh. It collapsed when the banana leader was hurt."

"Violence?"

"No, no. On the way to a negotiating session he slipped on a people skin."

"Why don't you want to talk about the *Sweathog?*" Julie asked.

"I have a strange feeling about it," Kotter replied. "A feeling that all is not quite right."

"You mean you think this edition is going to flop too?"

"No, not that. Maybe it's because the sweathogs seem to be doing everything right. They're getting out on the streets, reporting on what's going on. That's not how the sweathogs usually work. They look for the easy way, the gimmick. I find it hard to believe that they've reformed."

"But you've heard the phone ringing constantly, the stories coming in," Julie said.

"I know," Kotter said, nodding. "Still, I have that strange feeling."

"Well, we'll find out," Julie said. "Today's the day."

Kotter winced. "Did you have to use those words?"

"What's the matter?"

"That's exactly what the head banana said when he left the bunch to go to that negotiating session."

When Kotter reached the school, Horshack was at the main entrance selling the *Sweathog.* And the students were buying, crowding around him, snatching papers as fast as he could pass them out.

"Extra! Get your hotcake! Extra! Extra!" Horshack was chanting.

"Hotcake?" Kotter asked, buying a paper.

"That's what they're selling like, Mr. Kotter."

Extricating himself from the crush of students around Horshack, Kotter walked on toward his classroom. On the way, he met Charley Piper, who was clutching a copy of the *Sweathog* and grinning elatedly.

"Have you read it?" Piper said. "It's packed!"

"No, I haven't read it yet. Packed with what?"

"Human tragedy, crime and sex!" Piper said, walking along with him toward the classroom. "Wait'll you read about the woman who for years has been existing on food stamps."

"What's news about that?"

"She doesn't know that they can be used to buy food, she eats the stamps," Piper explained. "Is that human tragedy or is that human tragedy?"

"It makes me feel guilty," Kotter said. "I didn't finish my raisin this morning."

"Do you know that the biggest fence in the country has his headquarters right here in this neighborhood?" Piper said. "It's right here in the paper."

"How big a fence is he? Bigger than the Great Wall of China?"

"Not that kind of fence. The kind of fence who deals in stolen goods."

"Who is it?" Kotter asked. "Anybody I know? One of my students?"

"The story doesn't say."

"It doesn't say who the fence is? Then how do you know the story is true?"

"It's right here in the paper," Piper replied, "in black and white."

"Does it say who the woman is who eats food stamps?" Kotter asked, as they reached the door to his classroom and halted.

Piper opened the paper and read. "No, it doesn't mention her name. But it's a great human interest story." He turned to the front page. "And here's an editorial on it. It says the government ought to provide the people who get food stamps with either clearer instructions or syrup."

"Syrup?"

"To put on the food stamps if they eat them."

"Does the editorial mention the government by name?" Kotter asked.

"No. I read between the lines."

"I'm beginning to suspect that that's where the most news is in that paper—between the lines," Kotter said.

The first bell rang.

"Congratulate the sweathogs for me," Piper said, walking on.

"I will. But I won't tell them who you are."

Kotter entered his classroom and sat down at his desk and began reading the *Sweathog*. It was indeed crammed with stories of human tragedy, crime and sex. One was about a man who had a winning number in the lottery, but who had left the lottery ticket in the glove compartment of his car, which had been stolen and then dumped into the East River. The man was not named. Another was about a woman (unidentified) whose flea circus, left to her by her late husband (unidentified), had been kidnapped and was being held for ransom, along with the dog (unidentified) which served as winter quarters for the circus. Still another story was about a man and woman (unnamed) who were carrying on a love affair aboard the subway system and who, according to witnesses (also unnamed), were going all the way—to the end of one of the subway lines (unidentified).

The second bell rang. A few moments later, the sweathogs arrived, babbling exultantly. They were unencumbered by unsold papers.

"Do I sniff the odor of the sweet smell of success?" Kotter said when they were seated.

"Man, we could have sold twice as many papers," Washington told him.

"Yeah, the ones we sold have already become collectors' items," Barbarino said. "They're selling second-hand for three times what they cost in the first place."

"I can believe it," Kotter said. "I had no idea that so many exciting things were going on in this neighborhood. Looking at the people I meet on the streets, it's hard to believe that they're the same people who are in the stories in the *Sweathog*. Of course," he added, "reading the paper doesn't make it any easier to believe that they're the same people—since no names are used."

"You noticed that, huh?" Washington said.

Kotter nodded. "The lovers who are riding the subway . . ." he began.

"We can't tell you who they are, Mr. Kotter," Horshack said. "We don't want to embarrass them."

"That's commendable. What I was wondering about

though is which subway line was it that they went all the way to the end of?"

"Subways have feelings too, Mr. Kotter. We don't want to embarrass the subway line either."

"I see." Kotter looked down at the paper, which was still open on his desk. "Any late bulletin on this kidnapping of this woman's winter quarters?" he asked.

"It's the fleas' winter quarters," Epstein said. "It's the woman's dog." He shook his head. "Nothing new on that."

"What's the reason for not using her name?" Kotter asked.

"The kidnappers warned her that if she talked to the papers or the cops something would happen to the fleas," Washington explained.

"But, obviously, she *did* talk to the papers," Kotter said. "The story is right here."

"Yeah, but as long as we didn't use her name, she can tell the kidnappers that story is about some *other* woman who's had her fleas kidnapped," Washington said.

Kotter nodded. "That makes sense. It's a common occurrence. You can't pick up a paper or turn on the radio these days without reading about or hearing about a flea kidnapping." He looked down at the paper again. "And this story about the man and the lottery ticket . . ."

"That's not all true, Mr. Kotter," Barbarino said.

"Aha!"

"The car didn't get stolen," Barbarino said. "The man pushed it in the East River himself. It was junk. But if we'd used his name in the paper the cops could've got him for littering."

"Uh-huh."

"Besides that, how do you like the paper, Mr. Kotter?" Vernajean asked.

"Well . . . at first, I liked it very much. It seemed to have everything a newspaper reader could ask for."

"Human tragedy, crime and sex!" Horshack said.

"Exactly," Kotter agreed. "And then I began to have a sense of unfullfillment. It was like I was eating cotton candy and I suddenly realized that something was wrong. It *looked* like cotton candy. It *felt* like cotton candy. But it wasn't. It was cotton—no candy."

"Mr. Kotter, you're not supposed to eat the paper, you're supposed to read it," Horshack said.

"Maybe you just got a bad copy," Washington said. He reached for the paper on Kotter's desk. "Let me taste it."

"What I'm saying is that the real flavor of the paper—the names—is missing," Kotter said. "The stories are . . . well, the stories are no worse than the stories in most papers. But they leave me unsatisfied. I want to know who. Who! Who! Who!"

"We're protecting our sources," Washington said.

"Pardon?"

"You take that man that pushed his junk car in the river," Washington said. "If we used his name in the story, he might guess who told us. And he might get mad at the guy for telling us and punch him out. But this way, without the name, the guy that shoved his car in the river can't even prove the story's about him."

"Perfectly logical," Kotter said. He smiled benignly. "I apologize," he said.

"For what, Mr. Kotter?" Horshack asked.

Washington glared at Horshack. "Why'd you have to ask that?" he said. "Now, here comes the load."

"I apologize for what I was thinking," Kotter said. "I had a picture in my mind of a bunch of reporters sitting around the pool hall phoning in fictitious stories to the newspaper office. These reporters had figured out that if they didn't use names in the stories, then the stories couldn't be checked."

The sweathogs all looked in other directions, some toward the windows, some toward the ceiling, others down at the floor.

"But *now* I understand," Kotter went on. "These reporters were really just protecting their sources."

"Hey, we better get our books together," Washington said to the others. "The bell's going to ring."

"It will be another twenty minutes before the bell rings," Kotter said. "Let's discuss the *Sweathog* a little more. I realize that you had a bad experience with the first edition. And for good reason. It was a rip-off. Even worse, it was dull. But . . ."

The door flew open and Mr. Woodman, the assistant principal, came bursting into the room waving a copy of the *Sweathog*.

"I'm suing!" Woodman raged. "I get a retraction or I'm suing!"

Kotter stared at him in amazement. "So you're the one who's riding the subway!" He winked. "You can tell me, Mr. Woodman—which line is it?"

"Not *that* story!" Woodman fumed.

"Oh. Sorry." Kotter shrugged. "Well, at least, now I know what happened to that old car you used to drive. Sorry about the lottery ticket."

"Not *that* story either!"

"You're a bigger fence than the Great Wall of China?" Kotter guessed.

"Not that— What are you talking about? I didn't read any story on the Great Wall of China!"

"Mr. Woodman," Washington said, "you're not in any story in there."

"Don't try a cover-up on me!" Woodman shouted. "I know when I've been slandered! The story on the corruption in the school system! That's me!"

"Are we about to hear a confession?" Kotter asked.

"No! It's not about me! But everybody who's anybody in the school system will *think* it's about me. 'A bigwig'—that's what it says!"

"And you think that's you?" Kotter said.

"I can read between the lines, Kotter!"

"Your problem isn't slander, your problem is delusions of grandeur," Kotter told him.

"Yeah, you don't even wear a wig, Mr. Woodman," Washington said.

"But it's *my* supply closet that's being systematically looted of paper clips!" Woodman said. "And this story on the paper clip caper points the finger straight at me!"

"How so?" Kotter asked.

"I have the opportunity," Woodman replied. "The supply closet is right across from my office. And I often work late. After everyone else has gone, I could easily slip into that supply closet and make off with those paper clips."

"And motive too," Kotter said. "I've noticed that when you get excited you calm yourself by straightening paper clips." He winked again. "Was the supply at home running low?"

"See what I mean!" Woodman said victoriously. "You read that story and you think it was me. You're my witness, Kotter!" He faced the sweathogs again. "I demand a retraction—or I sue!"

"How can we retraction you?" Washington responded indignantly.

"Yeah—how?" the others wanted to know.

"Why can't you?" Kotter asked them.

"We don't know what retraction means," Barbarino said.

"It means that in the next edition you'll carry a story saying Mr. Woodman isn't the paper clip thief," Kotter explained.

"We can't do that," Washington said. "We didn't think it was him when we put in the story. But, now . . . I don't know . . . he's got the opportunity and the motive. How can we say he isn't the thief when maybe he is?"

Woodman exploded. "I'll sue!"

"How can you sue?" Washington asked. "Your name wasn't in that story."

" 'Bigwig,' it said!"

"You're not very big either, Mr. Woodman," Epstein said. "What are you, about five-six?"

"Mr. Woodman, they're right—your name wasn't used in the story," Kotter said. "I don't think you can sue for what you read between the lines."

"If I can't do that, then I'll shut the *Sweathog* down!" he raged. "This school is not big enough for two newspapers. The *Booster* is all the newspaper the students need!"

"Ahhhhhh . . ." Kotter said, smiling. "It's not what

you read between the lines, it's the competition that bothers you."

"Competition!" Woodman said derisively. "The *Sweathog* is no competition for the *Booster!*"

"The *Sweathog* sells like hotcakes," Kotter countered. "What does the *Booster* sell like?"

"Man, even giving the *Booster* away, it sells like measles infections," Washington said.

"The *Booster* has scruples!" Woodman said.

"What's that?" Barbarino asked.

"It's cockroaches," Epstein told him. "They're everywhere."

"The *Sweathog* is . . ." Woodman charged, red-faced, "is . . . is . . . the *Sweathog* is a scandal sheet!" He took in a deep breath, calming himself. "There—I said it!"

"Take it easy—you're getting yourself all worked up," Kotter said. "Want a paper clip to straighten?"

Woodman reached into his pocket. "No, I have a supply right here." He suddenly realized what he was saying. His face began turning red again. "I'll close down the *Sweathog* if it's the last thing I ever do!" he bellowed, stomping from the room.

The door slammed.

"Can he do that, Mr. Kotter?" Washington asked, concerned.

"Shut down your paper?" Kotter sat down at his desk again. "I don't know."

"Well, one thing," Barbarino said, "we know we're putting out a good paper now. If Mr. Woodman hates it, it must be great."

"Let's talk about that," Kotter said. "Do you know what innuendo is?"

"Isn't that the opposite of out-uendo?" Horshack said.

"When I was a little kid, my mother used to say a poem about that," Barbarino said. "It went 'in and out uendo, in and out uendo . . .' I don't remember the rest of it."

"Let me start again," Kotter said. "That story about the lovers and the subway. Now, everybody who read the paper thinks they know who those two are. And they all probably have somebody different in mind. That means that if, say, ten people read the story, ten different couples are being accused—in the readers' minds—of being the lovers in the story. So, at least nine of those couples are being unfairly accused."

"Is this a math lesson, Mr. Kotter?" Horshack asked.

"No, it's a lesson in scruples."

"Darn!" Horshack said. "If it was a math lesson, I had the answer. It was seven, wasn't it?"

"Dummy up, Horshack," Epstein said. "We're talking about cockroaches."

"We're talking about fairness," Kotter said. "If you weren't going to use the names, you had no right to carry that story."

"Mr. Kotter, we told you why we didn't use the names," Washington said. "We didn't want to embarrass nobody."

"What about these other stories," Kotter said, looking down at the paper again. "For instance, this story on Moose Regan and the false alarm. In here, you refer to Moose as 'the occupant of the phone booth.' Why didn't you use his name?"

"That was another time where we had to protect our source," Washington explained.

"Your source? Your source was your reporter. Epstein called that story in."

"Yeah, we had to protect Epstein from Moose," Washington said.

"He saw me in that other phone booth," Epstein told Kotter. "If we used his name, he'd kill me."

"I don't see what's wrong, Mr. Kotter," Washington said. "Man, we're a big success. We got the *Booster* on the run."

"You're not being professional," Kotter told them. "When a regular newspaper carries a story it names names."

Washington shook his head. "No, it don't."

"That's right, Mr. Kotter," Horshack said. "Remember that newspaper you showed us and told us that was the way a newspaper ought to be run? We learned a lot from that."

"Yeah, there was a story about the Russians cheating in the arms race," Epstein said. "And the guy they got the story from, they didn't use his name. Unless somebody is named 'an official in the State Department.' "

"And there was a story on unemployment," Washington said, "and the only name mentioned was some guy called 'a member of the cabinet who refused to be quoted.' "

"And there's some blabbermouth named 'a high official' who runs around all over the country giving out stories to the papers," Barbarino said. "He was in California on one page and in Maine on another and out in Chicago on another. You know who I think that guy is? That's Superman. But the paper didn't use his name."

"They didn't dare," Washington said. "He'd go through them like a speeding bullet."

"So what was that you were saying, Mr. Kotter?" Horshack asked.

"I just wanted to compliment you on how professional you are," Kotter replied.

The bell rang.

"How would you like to have a story in the *Sweathog* about you being the best teacher in the school, Mr. Kotter?" Washington said, as the sweathogs rose and moved toward the door.

"What good would that do? Nobody would know who the story was about."

"We could use your name."

Kotter shook his head. "Thanks, anyway. But it wouldn't be professional."

When the sweathogs had gone, Kotter went to the door, waiting for his next class to arrive.

Charley Piper came along, looking oddly subdued. "Gabe," he said, "there's something I've got to tell you. It's been on my mind ... I've got to tell someone about it ..."

"What is it?"

"That story in the *Sweathog* ... about the lovers ... about the subway ..."

"Yes?"

"The story, you know, about the guy and the girl ... going all the way to the end of the line ..."

"Yes, I know, I know," Kotter said. "What about it?" He suddenly brightened. "You mean ..."

"Shhhh!"

Kotter lowered his voice. "You mean you . . ."

"Yes, me," Piper said. "I *wish* I was that guy."

Kotter grinned. He gave Piper a knowing poke in the ribs. "You dog, you!" he said.

FIVE

"You've said exactly seven words this morning," Julie said to Gabe, sitting across from him at the kitchen table.

"Does that include 'ouch' when I bumped my elbow on the door frame?"

"No. But it *does* include 'Good morning,' which shouldn't count," Julie replied. "So, that makes only five words. Gabe, what's wrong? Have we been married longer than I realize? Have we reached the stage where we only speak to each other in the morning when it's absolutely necessary?"

Kotter frowned thoughtfully. "What would be absolutely necessary?" he asked.

"Well, for instance, if I'd hidden the sugar and you needed sugar for your cereal, you'd have to ask me for the sugar."

"Why would you hide the sugar?"

"To get you to talk to me. To get you to say, at least, 'Where's the sugar?' "

"Then, no, we haven't reached that stage," Kotter said. "I feel confident in saying that because the sugar bowl is sitting right there in plain view on the table."

"That wasn't really the question," Julie said. "The question was: What's wrong?"

Kotter suggested an explanation. "I got hold of the tube of glue this morning instead of the toothpaste and my jaws are stuck together?"

Julie shook her head. "It's not only you, it's the apartment too," she said. "It's so *quiet*. Lately, at least one of the sweathogs is usually here by this time doing some work on the paper before school. But listen!"

Kotter listened. "It's beautiful," he said. "No jangling phone. No peck, peck, peck of the typewriter."

"It's terrifying!" Julie said. "I'm used to living in a newspaper office. This place sounds like a home."

"You ought to make a tape of the sweathogs at work and then play it back when they're not here," Kotter said.

"Gabe, stop. Tell me what's wrong."

"Well . . . I intended to wait until it's all over."

"Until what's all over?"

"The crunch," he said. "Mr. Woodman is trying to shut down the *Sweathog*. He's summoned us to a hearing this morning. A lawyer from the board of education will be there. Evidently, Mr. Woodman has some legal step in mind. What, I don't know."

Julie looked stunned. "*Why* does he want to shut down the *Sweathog*?"

"He says it's because he's been slandered. He claims that—between the lines—he was accused of being the paper clip thief in that story in the *Sweathog*. But that's not the real reason. He doesn't like the competition the *Sweathog* is giving the *Booster*."

"That's terrible!" Julie said indignantly. "Can he really stop the sweathogs from putting out their paper?"

"I don't know. It depends on what the lawyer has to say."

"Do the sweathogs have a lawyer too?"

Kotter shook his head. "Only me."

Julie looked despairing for a moment, then brightened slightly. "We'll win," she said. "You're as good as any lawyer. You'll think of something."

"I've already thought of something," Kotter told her. "I plan to plead guilty and ask for five years in solitary."

"You're not on trial."

"I know, but it'll get me away from the jangle of the phone and the constant peck, peck, peck of the typewriter."

Kotter and the sweathogs arrived first at the conference room where they were to meet with Mr. Woodman and the lawyer.

"I got our defense all planned, Mr. Kotter," Barbarino said. "We're pleading insanity."

"How will that keep the *Sweathog* in business?"

"They'll put Mr. Woodman away," Barbarino replied. "We're claiming he's the one who's nuts."

"How do you plan to prove it?"

"We'll show the lawyer Mr. Woodman's pocketful of paper clips," Barbarino said. "Anybody who can't get through the day without straightening a pocketful of paper clips has got a problem." He tapped his skull. "Up here."

At that moment, Mr. Woodman and the lawyer arrived. The lawyer was a tall, middle-aged man, with an extremely pale complexion. He introduced himself as Oscar Wattling. Meeting the sweathogs had a discomfiting effect on him. During the introductions he kept fortifying himself with small red pills.

"Nerves," he explained, popping another pill.

"There went our defense," Barbarino said. "Straightening paper clips is nothing."

When they were all seated around the conference table, Oscar Wattling addressed the group. "Let it be understood that this is not a kangaroo court," he said to Kotter and the sweathogs. "I am not here to represent Mr. Woodman. I am here to represent the school board."

"I accept that," Woodman said. "I'm in the right in this and right is might."

"Our object," Oscar Wattling went on, "is to avoid controversy—the kind of controversy that can get into the newspapers." He lowered his voice. "The papers are after us, you know," he said. He popped another pill. "They *love* to make us look bad. Why, a thing like this—what the papers would call censorship—could . . ." He shuddered. "Before the meeting begins, I think we all ought to take an oath that nothing that is said here will get to the papers."

"That's censorship," Kotter pointed out.

"Well then, let's agree that if we do talk to the papers we'll all say the same thing," Wattling said. "We'll put up a solid front."

"What would you like to have us say?" Kotter asked.

"Just say 'no comment.'"

"I like that," Woodman said. "It sums it up very well."

Kotter shook his head. "We can't agree to anything like that in advance," he said.

Wattling popped another pill. "I knew this was going to be that kind of day when I woke up this morning," he said. "I fell out of the wrong side of the bed." He turned to Woodman. "Very well, let's begin. What are the charges?"

"Number one, slander," Woodman said. "The *Sweathog* as much as accused me of being a paper clip thief. My reputation is at stake," he said. "Are my years of dedicated and devoted service to education to go for naught? Am I to be crucified on the cross of yellow journalism?" Trembling, he got a paper clip from his pocket and began straightening it. "Am I to be . . ."

Wattling interrupted. "Would you mind not playing with that paper clip," he said. He popped another pill. "It makes me nervous."

"I am not *playing!*" Woodman replied huffily. "I'm just trying to stay calm. And the reason I'm *not* calm is because you make *me* nervous with those pills."

"You could use some of these pills yourself," Wattling said. "If you took pills, you wouldn't need paper clips."

"If you used paper clips, you wouldn't need pills!" Woodman countered.

"At least, I got my pills honestly!" Wattling said.

"Are you accusing me of *stealing* these paper clips?"

"All I know is . . ."

"Gentlemen, please," Kotter said, breaking in. "Not in front of the students."

"Yeah, you could warp our little minds," Horshack said. "Hahh . . . hahh . . . hahh . . ."

"Continue!" Wattling said sharply to Woodman.

"As I was saying, am I to be . . ."

"We've heard that," Wattling said. "Get to the facts." He groaned and popped another pill. "Thank God there are only three-hundred-and-sixty-five days in the year. Three-hundred-and-sixty-six and I'd be on blue pills too."

"Those *are* the facts," Woodman said. "The paper accused me of stealing paper clips."

"His name wasn't in the story," Washington said.

"It was!" Woodman said. "You accused a 'bigwig!' "

"We rest our case," Kotter said quickly. "An assistant principal is not a bigwig."

"Charge dismissed," Wattling said. He sighed happily. "I did it! I got through a whole case without once breaking into tears."

"The case isn't over," Woodman told him. "That was only the *first* charge."

There was a sudden wetness in Wattling's eyes. "All right," he said sorrowfully, "go on."

"The *Sweathog* is disruptive," Woodman said.

"How?" Kotter asked.

"The students stand around in the corridors reading it," Woodman said. "They should be thinking about their studies."

"They didn't stand around in the corridors thinking about their studies *before* the *Sweathog* came out," Kotter said. "They stood around in the corridors reading comic books."

"Then the newspaper is an improvement," Wattling said.

"Ahhhh ... I wouldn't say that," Kotter said. "But it's something different."

"Charge dismissed," Wattling said.

"I'm not finished," Woodman said.

A tear trickled down Wattling's cheek. He popped a pair of pills.

"The *Sweathog* encourages crime," Woodman charged. "It instructs its readers in the ways and means of turning in false fire alarms."

"If it does that," Kotter said, "then it also instructs them to drop their cigars in their pockets while they're calling in the false alarm and then get caught by the firemen."

"And get washed down into the subway by the hoses," Washington added.

"Charge dismissed," Wattling said.

"I object!" Woodman raged.

"Objection overruled!" Wattling broke into a big smile. "I sounded just like a judge when I said that, didn't I?" The smile softened. "I'd *like* to be a judge," he said. "When the arguing started, I could call a recess and go into my quarters and take my pills in private." He sighed wistfully. "We all have our little dreams."

"Are we finished?" Kotter asked.

"No. I have to render my decision." Wattling looked at Kotter narrowly. "If I rule against you and make these students stop publishing their paper, will you go to the *real* newspapers and complain about censorship?" he asked.

"Very likely."

"I suspected that." He turned to Woodman. "If I rule against you and let the students continue publishing their paper, will you try to make trouble for me by taking your case to a higher authority, say my superior?" he asked.

"I just might do that!" Woodman told him.

"Even though you realize that I have a certain influence with the powers that be and might get you transferred to Staten Island?" Wattling asked him.

Woodman winced. "*The* Staten Island? Across the river?"

Wattling nodded. "The Staten Island that's almost as far away as New Jersey."

"That might make a difference," Woodman conceded.

"Then I rule in favor of the *Sweathog*," Wattling said. He popped another pair of pills. "It's over!" he said thankfully. "I did it!"

The sweathogs cheered.

Holding his breath, Woodman began frantically straightening a paper clip.

"I don't like to see this end this way," Kotter said.

"Didn't you hear him?" Washington said. "We won!"

"Yes, but the bad feeling still exists," Kotter said. He addressed Woodman. "There's still a way for you to close down the *Sweathog*," he said.

"Somebody got to our lawyer!" Barbarino said.

"If it weren't for the way you run the *Booster*," Kotter said, still addressing Woodman, "there would be no reason for the *Sweathog* to exist. Why do you think the sweathogs started their paper?"

"They're out to get me!" Woodman charged.

"No," Kotter said.

"I thought that was the reason too," Barbarino said.

"Because the *Booster* doesn't represent the students," Kotter told Woodman, "it represents you. *You* decide what goes into it. And you make that decision on the basis of what you think the students *ought* to read, not what they want to read. As a result, it's a dull, out-of-touch paper."

"That's the same as saying that *I* am dull and out-of-touch!" Woodman replied. "I challenge that, Kotter! Prove it!"

"That last issue of the *Booster* carried a story that blamed juvenile delinquency on the Twist," Kotter said. "Do you have any idea how long it's been since anybody danced the Twist?"

"Ah, the good old days," Wattling said. "That was when a man could get elected to public office merely by promising to get that dance banned." He popped another pill. "Things aren't that simple these days," he complained. "I'm thinking of running for office myself, but I don't know whether to be *for* pot or against it."

"The solution, it seems to me," Kotter said, continuing to address Woodman, "is for you to give up your throttle hold on the *Booster*. Let the students run it."

Woodman drew back, going pale, appalled by the idea that Kotter had suggested.

"Then there would be no need for the *Sweathog*," Kotter told him.

"Wait a minute!" Washington said. "Mr. Kotter, whose side are you on?"

"On the side of reason—I hope."

"*That* will get you nowhere," Wattling told him. "I

know—I've tried it. I warn you—stick to reason and you'll soon be on pills."

"The *Sweathog* is a success!" Epstein said to Kotter. "It's the biggest thing since . . . since . . . since . . ."

"Since the Twist," Wattling said helpfully.

"And you're trying to kill it!" Epstein said to Kotter.

"Not kill it. What I'm suggesting is a merger." Kotter turned back to Woodman. "What do you say?"

Woodman sputtered, speechless.

"I know what I say," Washington said, rising. "I'm walking!" He strode toward the door.

Epstein, Horshack and Barbarino got up too and headed for the exit.

"The *Sweathog* lives!" Barbarino cried out defiantly as they followed Washington from the conference room.

When the sweathogs had gone, Wattling held out his bottle of pills to Kotter. "Have one."

Kotter shook his head. "It hasn't reached that point yet," he said. He turned to Woodman again. "But I'll take one of those paper clips," he said.

Dinner that evening in the Kotter kitchen was accompanied by sounds of the sweathogs at work on the next edition of the paper in the living room. Every few minutes the telephone rang. The click of typewriter keys was constant. Between rings of the phone the door slammed, as one or another of the paper's reporters arrived or departed. There were loud arguments about which stories belonged on which pages. And every once in a while one of the sweathogs would appear in the kitchen for a fresh supply of snacks from the refrigerator and cupboard.

"Enough!" Kotter said finally.

"Gabe . . . temper, temper . . ." Julie said.

"I can't live this way!" he said.

"It *is* getting to be a bit much," Julie agreed. "At first, it was fun. Now, it's just noise."

"I'm going to throw them out," Kotter said, rising from the table.

"Gabe—no! Talk to them. Explain it to them," Julie said. "Tell them we love having them, but . . . well, tell them that . . ." She frowned. "Maybe it would be better to write them a note."

"And read it in the *Sweathog?* Everything that comes into this apartment goes into that paper. They don't care what it is. The milkman stuck an advertisement for half-and-half under the door this morning and tonight Vernajean is writing it up as a story."

"All right, talk to them," Julie said. "But be gentle."

Kotter took a moment to calm himself, then entered the living room.

"Kids . . ." he said, standing in the center of the room.

No one noticed. The typing went on. The telephoning continued. Horshack entered, slamming the door, and Epstein departed, slamming the door.

Kotter approached Horshack. "I know you're busy," he said.

"Later, Mr. Kotter," Horshack said. "I got to go pick up the ad for the supermarket." He departed, slamming the door.

A second later, Epstein returned, slamming the door.

"That door," Kotter said to Epstein. "It's only human. Do unto others as you would have others do unto you."

Epstein stared at him puzzledly.

"How would you like to be slammed every two minutes?" Kotter asked him.

Epstein brightened. "That's a great story," he said. "Lots of human interest. Thanks, Mr. Kotter." He went to a table and began scribbling furiously on a pad. "Hold the typewriter!" he called out to Washington. "Big door story—coming up!"

"What kind of a door story?" Washington asked.

"A *human* door!" Epstein told him.

"Hey—wow! Front page!"

Kotter walked over to where Washington was seated at the typewriter. "Could you spare me a minute?" he asked.

Washington stopped typing. "Sure, Mr. Kotter."

"Living in this apartment is unbearable," Kotter told him. "We . . ."

"Hold it, Mr. Kotter," Washington said. He called over to Epstein. "Hold the door story," he said. "Come on over here and get Mr. Kotter's story. He's gonna get a bear for the apartment."

"No!" Kotter said.

"Kill the bear!" Washington called out to Epstein. "He changed his mind." He looked up at Kotter again. "You're right," he said. "We wouldn't get any work done around here. We'd be stumbling over that bear all the time."

Horshack returned, slamming the door.

"*That* is what I mean!" Kotter said. "That's what makes living in this apartment unbearable. That door, slamming, slamming, slamming."

Washington nodded. "We need a new door—one

that swings both ways," he said. "You want to handle that, Mr. Kotter?"

"The door stays," Kotter told him. "It's the slammers who are going!"

Vernajean, on the phone, called over to him. "Mr. Kotter, if you're going to shout, will you go in the kitchen, please?" she said. "This is an important call."

Epstein dropped the handwritten story on the human door on the typewriter stand. "Clean this up," he said to Washington. "I'm going over to pick up the ad for McNary's Pharmacy."

Epstein departed, slamming the door.

"This racket is driving us out of our home!" Kotter told Washington. "And it's not just that! The food! Our grocery bill has tripled! Tripled!"

Horshack stopped by. "What's that, a baseball story?" he asked. "The season hasn't even started yet."

"It's a food story," Washington told him.

"If it's the food stamp angle, no go," Horshack said. "We've already covered that." He left again, slamming the door.

"Mr. Kotter," Washington said, "I know what you're talking about. This probably isn't easy for you and Mrs. Kotter, all the racket we make out here. And you don't even get to get any private phone calls any more, 'cause we got the phone tied up. And, man, it must cost you a fortune, all the groceries we eat up."

Kotter beamed. "You *do* understand!"

"Yeah, I got a head, I can figure things out," Washington said. "So, listen, Mr. Kotter, just don't worry about it any more. I'll take care of it."

"I appreciate that, Washington."

"Yeah, I know how you feel, man. After all, this is your home."

"Right. No hard feelings."

"Nahhhhh . . ." ˋ

"What exactly are you going to do about it?" Kotter asked.

"The fair thing," Washington replied, turning back to the typewriter. "As soon as the paper starts making big money, we'll give you a little something to cover expenses." He looked up at Kotter again. "Do you think you could get us a new typewriter?" he said. "The 'e' key on this one sticks."

"N v r!" Kotter replied, storming from the room.

In the kitchen, fuming, Kotter paced—from the refrigerator to the sink, from the sink to the cupboard, from the cupboard to the refrigerator, and so on. The sounds from the living room—door slamming, typewriting, arguing, telephoning—continued.

"Did they throw you out?" Julie asked.

"They have taken over!" Kotter said. "They can't do that! This is my home!"

"And a man's home is his castle," Julie said, nodding. "What did they say to you?"

"Washington offered to 'give me a little something for expenses' once the paper is making big money."

Julie looked surprised. "That's better than I expected," she said. "I thought they might try to charge us rent for living behind their newspaper office. Did you accept?"

"Accept? I came in here to calm down a bit," Kotter replied. "Then, I'm going back in there and throw them out!" He raised a hand to stifle any protest that Julie might intend to make. "Don't try to talk me out of it. I've made up my mind. Door-slammers—that's them—and men of gentle ways—that's me—cannot coexist in the same small apartment."

"There's an idea," Julie said. "We could move to a larger apartment and leave them here."

"No. Out they go." He halted and took a deep breath. "I'm all right now, I'm calm," he said. "I'm going in there and throw them out."

"Gently, oh, man of gentle ways," Julie said.

"Right, gently. I'll just grab them— I mean, I'll just take them by the hands and lead them to the door and give them a shove that— No, kill the shove. I'll give them my best, that's what I'll give them. I'll give them my best and tell them that anytime they want to come back as visitors, they'll be welcome. I'll tell them that, personally, I hope they understand why I'm doing what I'm doing. As I said to Washington earlier, 'No hard feelings.' After all, they're old enough to realize that there are times when people need a little quiet. That's one of the reasons why I have a home, I'll tell them, so I can get away from the hustle and bustle, the hurry and scurry. On the other hand, I'll say, I also understand their need to create their newspaper in an atmosphere of throbbing, pulsing excitement. After all, the newspaper business . . ."

Julie interrupted. "You're not going to *throw* them out," she said, "you're going to bore them out."

"You're right. I'm beginning to sound like Mr. Woodman." Kotter straightened, scowling darkly. "The thing to do is to do it," he said, heading back toward the living room. "I'll just go in there and . . ."

"Gabe—wait!" Julie said.

He halted. "What now?"

"Listen! Do you hear that?"

Kotter cocked an ear. "I don't hear anything."

"That's what I mean. What happened to all the noise?"

Kotter considered for a moment, still scowling. "Maybe they *did* understand what I was saying," he said. "Maybe they've left." He shook his head. "I can't believe that." He moved on to the kitchen doorway and peeked into the living room. "Oh-oh!"

Quickly, Julie got up from the table and joined him.

Two enormous men were standing just inside the apartment doorway. They had closed the door behind them and they were looking threateningly at the sweathogs, who, in turn, were staring at the men in stunned alarm.

"Who are they?" Julie whispered to Kotter.

"I don't know their names," he replied. "But I've seen enough movies to know what they are. They're hoods."

"Call the police!"

"They have the telephone." Kotter pointed out. He forced a small smile. "Maybe I'm wrong, maybe they're not hoods. Maybe they stopped in to buy advertising in the *Sweathog*."

"They don't look like buyers."

"Well, steal some advertising, then. Let's find out," Kotter said, moving on.

As he and Julie entered the living room, one of the men whipped out a pistol.

"Movies never lie," Kotter said. "Those are hoods."

"Who're you?" the man with the gun asked him.

"I live here," Kotter answered. He nodded toward

the kitchen. "In there, right behind the newspaper office," he said.

The man grunted gruffly and put the pistol away. "Is dis da place where dat crummy paper comes from?" he asked.

"Dis is da place," Kotter replied.

"Is youse da guys dat put out da crummy paper?" the man asked.

Kotter indicated the sweathogs. "Dey is," he said.

The hood looked at the sweathogs threateningly. "I got news for youse," he told them.

"Hey—a story!" Washington said, looking somewhat relieved.

"It ain't no story," the hood told him. "It's a message. It's from Lousy Louie. You put it in da paper dat Lousy Louie lives in dis neighborhood. Lousy Louie don't like dat."

"Lousy Louie?" Kotter said. "Are you sure you have the right newspaper? I don't remember reading anything about anyone named Lousy Louie in the *Sweathog.*"

"It didn't say Lousy Louie in da paper. It said da biggest fence in da country."

"If we didn't use his name," Washington said, "how did he know it was him?"

"He read between the lines," Kotter said. "There's a lot of that going around."

"Lousy Louie don't read," the hood said. "How he knew it was him in da paper was because Lousy Louie is da biggest fence in da country."

"Then why does he object to the story?" Kotter asked. "It was free advertising."

"Lousy Louie don't want no advertising," the hood

said. "He says da guys dat do business with him, dey *know* where he lives. And da guys dat don't do business with him—like da cops—he don't want 'em to know where he lives." He looked threateningly at the sweathogs again. "Has you paper guys got dat in your heads?"

"Yeah, it's clear, it's clear!" Washington said.

"Just a minute," Kotter said, addressing the hood. "I can understand your concern. But Lousy Louie's name was *not* used in the paper. So, as far as your complaint is concerned, I don't think you have a leg to stand on."

"Funny you should mention not having a leg to stand on," the hood replied. "Because if Lousy Louie is put in dis paper again, dat's what everybody on da paper is gonna have—not a leg to stand on."

"Are you saying . . ." Kotter began defiantly.

"Yeah, I'm saying," the hood told him. "If Lousy Louie is in da paper again, da guys on da paper is gonna get da wrong end of da pencil."

"The eraser end?" Washington guessed.

"You got it. Rubbed out." The first hood turned to the second hood. "Vincent," he said, "give dem a lesson on what occurs to guys dat crosses Lousy Louie."

The second hood picked up the typewriter. He lifted a leg, then smashed the typewriter across his knee, breaking it cleanly in two. That done, he placed the two halves back on the table.

"My typewriter!" Kotter moaned.

"The 'e' key was sticking anyway, Mr. Kotter," Washington said.

"And now we will take our leavings," the first hood said, opening the door. "But, like da good penny . . ."

"That's the 'bad' penny," Kotter said.

"Not in my crowd it ain't. We don't use dat word, bad. Nobody is bad, dey is just misunderstood. So, like da good penny, if Lousy Louie sees his name in da paper again, we shall return." He and the other hood stepped out into the corridor. "But da next time it won't be da machine dat gets broke in two," the first hood warned. "It will be da putter-outers of da paper. Youse won't be sweathogs no longer. Youse will be half sweats and half hogs."

The door closed.

There was dazed silence.

Then Washington poked a typewriter key. There was a click. "They fixed the 'e' key," Washington reported. "It doesn't stick."

"They can't do that, you know," Kotter said. "They can't come in here and tell you what stories you can and what stories you can't run in your paper. There's still freedom of the press."

The sweathogs began collecting their belongings.

"Where are you going?" Kotter asked.

"We're moving our office," Barbarino told him.

"We're going underground," Washington said.

"No, wait, you can't do that!" Kotter told them. "That would be giving in to intimidation."

"That's what we're doing," Epstein said, nodding.

Julie took Kotter aside. "This is what you wanted," she whispered. "You were going to throw them out—remember?"

"This is different," he said. "This is a matter of principle. If those thugs can dictate to the *Sweathog,* they can dictate to other papers. The sweathogs have got to keep their office right here in this apartment."

"Well, see you in school, Mr. Kotter," Washington said, going toward the door.

Kotter ran ahead of him and barred the way. "You can't leave!" he said. "Freedom of the press is at stake."

"Mr. Kotter, you heard what those hoods said. They'll break us in two. The sweats will be here working in the newspaper office, but where will the hogs be?"

"In the East River," Horshack said.

"Where will you go if you leave here?" Kotter asked.

There was silence again.

"Why don't we move into the subway," Horshack said finally. "According to the paper, there's a lot going on there."

"You couldn't work in the subway," Kotter said. "It's too crowded. Either you stay here or you give up your paper."

"And just when we were about to make some money," Washington said glumly.

"Okay, we stay," Barbarino said. "We just won't write any more stories about Lousy Louie."

"We didn't know we wrote a story about him the first time," Washington said. "We could do that again—write about him without knowing it."

"Then, how's this?" Barbarino said. "We make Mr. Kotter the publisher of the Sweathog."

"What good will that do?" Epstein asked.

"When those hoods come back to break us in two,"

Barbarino explained, "we say we don't know anything about it, we tell them to see the publisher."

"I *like* it!" Washington said. "Back to work!"

Moments later, the sweathogs were slaving away once more. Horshack departed, slamming the door. Vernajean was on the telephone. Epstein and Barbarino were arguing about the placement of a story, back page or front page. The only change was the absence of the clicking of the typewriter. Washington was writing with a pencil.

"Mrs. Kotter, you got any more of those cookies?" Vernajean called over from the phone.

"Coming up!" Julie answered, hurrying toward the kitchen.

Kotter trailed after her.

In the kitchen, while Julie placed cookies onto a plate, Kotter sank into a chair, looking totally shattered. "What have I done!" he moaned. "They were on their way out—and I *stopped* them!"

"That was *very* clever," Julie said.

"What?"

"You didn't fool me," she said. "You had it all planned, the whole thing. And it worked. Now ... you're a publisher!"

"Gabe Kotter, publisher of the *Sweathog*," he said dismally.

"It could lead to bigger and better things," Julie said.

"It could lead to a split!" Kotter said.

"A split? Us?" Julie said puzzledly.

"Not us. A split—me. I could end up Gabe Kotter, publisher, with the Gabe half in the East River and the Kotter half in the Hudson."

SIX

"I got word you want to see me," Epstein said, entering McNary's Pharmacy and addressing the owner, who, standing behind the counter, was wrapping a small package for delivery. "What's on, man?"

"About my advertising," McNary told him, circling the package with string.

"You already got your ad for this issue," Epstein said. "And your story too."

"Put your finger on the string," McNary said.

Epstein obeyed. "How come you use string?" he asked. "How come you don't use tape like everybody else?"

"I got a brother-in-law in the string business," McNary told him. "One hand washes the other—you know what I mean?" Having knotted the string, he picked up the package to inspect the job he had done. "Beautiful," he said. "If I could just mix prescriptions like I can tie bows, a lot of people would be a lot happier . . . may they rest in peace."

"What about your advertising?" Epstein asked.

"I like it," McNary said. "It's been good for my business. Only yesterday a customer mentioned my ad in the *Sweathog*. He came in clutching his chest, gasping for breath, saying he was having a heart attack. He wanted a prescription filled. So, while he waited, I asked him if he'd seen my ad, maybe that'd brought him in. He gasped yes. I asked him how he liked it. He gasped fine. I asked him if he read the story that went along with the ad."

"What'd he say?"

"Nothing. That was when I had to call the ambulance."

"Yeah, okay. But what about your advertising?" Epstein asked.

"I was thinking I might be smart to buy a whole year's ads in advance," McNary said.

"Hey—that's great!"

"That's what I was *thinking*," McNary said. "I haven't made up my mind yet. On the other hand, I might cancel my advertising in the *Sweathog* altogether."

"What for, man? You just told me it's doing you good. What about that man with the heart attack that came in because he saw your ad?"

McNary shrugged. "How do I know I can believe him? A man with a heart attack, a man who's dying, a man who needs a prescription fast . . . a man like that will say anything." He began filling out an address label for the package.

"What's gonna make you decide whether you buy more or cancel altogether?" Epstein asked.

"One hand washes the other," McNary said.

"Yeah, I dig," Epstein said. "You buy a whole year's advertising from us and we do something for you. What?"

"I've been thinking about the stories that go along with my ads," McNary said. He pasted the label on the package.

"You want *more* stories? *Two* stories for every ad?"

McNary shook his head. "What I was thinking about the stories is, I wonder how much good they do? Do they fool anybody? When the readers see my ad and my story there side by side, they probably say to themselves: the fix is on. So, they don't believe what they read in the story."

"Yeah, I get it. You want to drop the stories and just run the ads," Epstein said. "That's okay with us."

"I was thinking that would give you some extra space to do some crusading journalism," McNary said.

"Yeah, I guess we could do some of that," Epstein said disinterestedly.

"I got a *wonderful* crusading journalism story for you," McNary said. "You know the pharmacy up the street, my so-called competitor—I won't mention any names?"

"Finnery's, you mean?"

"That might be the name," McNary replied. "For the sake of discussion, we'll call it that—Finnery's. What a story that will be! An exposure! A blast! And you won't even have to go into the place and investigate, I can give you all the dirty details myself."

Epstein looked at him sideways. "You want a put-down on Finnery?" he said.

"It's not what *I* want," McNary replied. "It's what the aroused citizenry wants. Everywhere I go, people say to me, 'When is some crusading journalist going to tell the truth about what goes on at Finnery's?'"

"What *does* go on?" Epstein asked.

"High prices."

"Higher than yours?"

"That's a different story," McNary replied. "The story we're discussing now is the high prices at Finnery's—if that's the name."

"And what else?" Epstein asked.

"How do you know what you're getting at Finnery's?" McNary said. "Is it possible that you're getting prescriptions that do you more harm than good? Can it be true that Finnery doesn't wash his hands between prescriptions? How do we know that Finnery doesn't keep a goat in his store behind the counter? Is it true that goats carry diseases?"

"Those are all questions," Epstein said. "What're the answers?"

"It's the duty of a crusading newspaper to ask questions. It's the duty of Finnery to supply the answers—if he can."

"I get it," Epstein said. "You want us to run a story on Finnery's asking a lot of questions like that. Questions that'll make the readers think . . ."

McNary stopped him. "What the readers think is their own business," he said. "Who are we to tell people what to think? Truth, that's all that interests us. Let the pharmacy up the street fall where it may."

Epstein looked at him doubtfully. "Has Finnery really got a goat behind the counter?"

"It's what I'm told," McNary replied. "Twelve years ago a man came into my store. He was giving me his business, he said, because he didn't like that old goat behind the counter at Finnery's."

"What he meant . . ."

"Don't speak ill of the dead," McNary said, breaking in.

"The who?"

"Five years ago, that man who came into my store twelve years ago passed away. Don't call a man a liar who's not around to defend himself."

"About that story," Epstein said. "I wouldn't like to run a story like that, just questions."

"Well, it's a pleasant association we've had," McNary said. "Too bad it has to end this way, with me cancelling my advertising."

"Hey, wait a minute . . ."

"Maybe you want to think it over about the story," McNary said.

"Yeah, I guess I better talk to the other guys about it," Epstein decided.

"You do that," McNary said. "And mention it about the possibility of me taking a year's advertising in advance. And," he said, putting the wrapped package in Epstein's hands, "make a delivery for me, will you? The address in on the label."

Walking along the street alone, on his way to the newspaper office, Washington heard a sound that stopped him. He looked around, puzzled. Then he heard the sound again.

"Psssst!"

At the same time, Washington saw a man motioning to him from an alley. The man was big and nearly bald and was wearing an athletic jacket.

"Me?" Washington said, going to the entrance to the alley.

"Hi!" the man said amiably. "Remember me?"

Washington looked at him closely, then shook his head.

"I'm Coach Waters from Darby Academy. My team played your team last week. You beat the pants off us."

"Oh, yeah, I remember you," Washington said. "That was the team that kept shooting the ball into our basket. That's how come we beat you so bad. You run up our score for us."

"You're too modest," Coach Waters said. "You were the reason for our defeat. You played a great game."

"Yeah, well, I'm the star," Washington explained. "That's what the star does."

"I understand you've branched out," Coach Waters said.

Washington looked at himself. "Where?"

"No, I mean, I understand you're also writing sports for a newspaper now—the *Sweathog*."

"Yeah . . ."

"I'm going to level with you, Washington," Coach Waters said, "I'd like to have you on my team."

"I don't go to your school," Washington said.

"But that could be arranged. And you'd like it at Darby. It's a private school, you know. Very high class. And *very* expensive."

"I don't know . . . I like it where I am," Washington said. "It's low class. But I can afford it. It don't cost nothing."

"Have you ever heard of a scholarship? I could get you an athletic scholarship at Darby."

"With *my* grades, you could get me a scholarship?"

"I think I could guarantee you that at Darby you'd get top grades too," Waters told him.

Washington backed away from him a step. "Who're you really working for, some crazy scientist who wants to give me a brain transplant?"

"No, no," Coach Waters said. "I'm talking about an arrangement. Anything can be arranged, a scholarship, grades, anything." He smiled amiably again. "Of course, there are two sides to every arrangement."

"Uh-huh," Washington said, nodding. "What's my side."

Coach Waters' expression became woeful. "Washington, I don't want to be a high school level coach all my life," he said. "I long for the big time. College coaching. Then on to the pros."

"I haven't got a college," Washington said. "I can't hire you."

"No, you see, what I need is publicity. If I could just make a name for myself in high school coaching, I'd be in demand. The colleges would come to me."

"You already got kind of a name for yourself," Washington told him. "My own coach was talking about you at the game."

Waters brightened. "What did he say?"

"He said 'Why don't that dummy teach his kids which basket is theirs and which is ours?' "

"It's not my fault," Coach Waters said. "I tell them which basket is which, but they don't care. They're rich kids, you know. They can't be bothered with basketball scores, they're thinking about the stock market." His face fell again. "We don't have a team manager," he said, "we have a stock broker."

"What can I do for you?" Washington asked.

"You can do some stories on me in your newspaper," Coach Waters said. "Feature stories. Big stories—about how great a coach I am. Then I'll send those stories around to the colleges. That's what I need—publicity."

"Then, when that happens, I get the scholarship and the grades?" Washington said.

"It can be arranged."

Washington was silent.

"Well?" Coach Waters said.

"I'm trying to think of something good I could write about you as a coach," Washington replied. "It's not going to be easy."

"I have some old write-ups on Knute Rockne," Coach Waters said. "You can rework those. Just change it from football to basketball."

"I could do that," Washington replied.

"Then it's a deal?"

"I got to think about it," Washington told him.

"How long?"

"Give me a couple of weeks," Washington said. "I'll meet you right here two weeks from now. Same time, same alley."

"In the meantime," Coach Waters said, "I'll dig out those old stories on Knute Rockne."

"Yeah, and scratch out 'football' and write in 'basketball,' " Washington said. "I'm a star—I don't do my own scratching."

Walking along the school corridor alone, leaving to

go to the newspaper office, Barbarino heard a sound that stopped him. He looked around, puzzled. Then he heard the sound again.

"Pssssst!"

At the same time, Barbarino saw Mr. Woodman motioning to him from the doorway to his office.

"Me?" Barbarino said, going toward the doorway.

"Come in, come in," Woodman said nervously.

"Are you going to expel me?" Barbarino asked hopefully, entering the office. "What did I do this time?"

"No, this isn't anything like that," Woodman said. He gestured toward a chair. "Have a seat."

Barbarino was immediately suspicious. "You always make me stand up," he said.

"This is a different situation," Woodman told him. "Usually, when you're in here, Barbarino, it's for discipline. But this time it's for . . ." He swallowed hard, suddenly having difficulty speaking. "For a friendly chat." He got a paper clip from his pocket and began straightening it. "I plan to do more of this in the future . . . friendly chats with the students," he said. "I'll be a better assistant principal for it, I think, learning how the other half lives."

"Yeah, okay," Barbarino said. "I live in an apartment. There's me and my old man and my old lady and my brothers and sisters. Let's see . . . in the morning we eat breakfast . . ."

"No, that's not what I mean," Woodman said. "Actually, I thought we might discuss what we have in common. Newspapering, for instance. You know, despite what you might think, I admire the way you and your friends have handled the *Sweathog*. In fact, with a little guidance, I think, you could make it a big success."

"It's already a big success," Barbarino said.

"When I say 'big success,' I mean BIG success," Woodman told him. "There are awards given to school newspapers, you know. You might even win an award. And, if that happened, when you graduate from high school, you could take that award and walk into any big city newspaper in the country."

"And what?" Barbarino asked.

"Well, I can't be specific. I don't want to make any promises that the big city newspapers can't keep. I will say, however, that, under certain conditions, I would be willing to write you a glowing recommendation."

"What's the condition?" Barbarino asked.

"I was thinking . . . you and your friends and I really ought to team up."

"You want a job on the *Sweathog?*"

"That's not what I had in mind," Woodman replied, getting another paper clip from his pocket. "I was thinking more about . . . well, putting you and your friends in charge of the *Booster.*"

Barbarino thought for a moment. "If *that's* what you're thinking about, how come when Mr. Kotter said you ought to turn the *Booster* over to the students, you turned thumbs down?" he asked.

"What I'm suggesting is not exactly what I'm suggesting," Mr. Woodman replied. "I wouldn't be turning the *Booster* over to you and your friends. We'd be . . ." He swallowed hard again. "We'd be partners."

"But, a minute ago, you were talking about putting us in charge."

"Yes . . . in charge . . . in charge of the actual work

of putting out the paper. And I'd be in charge of ... well, in charge of guidance."

"Saying what went *in* the paper, you mean?"

"Yes, among other things. But, don't forget," he said quickly, "you'd get all the glory. You'd be the editors. You'd do the actual writing of the stories. And, when you finally graduate—if ever—you'd all leave here with glowing letters of recommendation."

"Yeah?" Barbarino said, tempted. "How glowing?"

"*Very* glowing," Woodman said. "You don't really know me, Barbarino. When I like a student—when a student obeys the rules—I can be *very, very* glowing."

Barbarino narrowed his eyes, studying Woodman closely. "Glow for me," he said.

"Laudatory, I mean," Woodman said. "I can be very complimentary."

"I don't know ..." Barbarino said. "I don't see how we could run two newspapers at the same time. You see, the problem is, we're tied up most of the day in classes."

"I didn't think of that," Woodman said, frowning. Then he immediately broke out in a small smile, which for Woodman was tantamount to a large smile. "I think I have the solution," he said. "You could give up the *Sweathog*."

"But it's our baby," Barbarino protested.

"Barbarino, if you're going to get ahead in this world, you can't let babies stand in your way," Woodman told him. "Think about it! Will your baby write you a glowing letter of recommendation?"

"You got a point," Barbarino conceded. "Who'd pay any attention to a letter from a baby anyway?"

"Talk to your friends about it," Woodman said. "I'm

sure they'll see the wisdom of dropping the *Sweathog* and working with me on the *Booster*."

"I'll let you know," Barbarino said, heading toward the door.

"Oh . . . and there's no need to mention this to Mr. Kotter," Woodman said. "Let's keep it as a surprise." His expression suddenly brightened. "And I want to be the one to tell him," he said eagerly.

When Barbarino reached the newspaper office, the other sweathogs were at work.

"I got a deal offered to me today," he told them.

"*You* got a deal!" Washington said. "I got a deal offered to me too. I was waiting for you to show up so I could tell everybody."

"Make that three deals," Epstein said. "I got one offered to me too."

"I had kind of a deal offered to me too," Horshack said. "I went over to the used car lot to try to sell some advertising. And the owner told me if I didn't get off his property he'd throw me off."

The apartment door opened and Kotter entered. He hesitated for a second, then deliberately slammed the door behind him.

"That's what it sounds like when you do it," he told the sweathogs.

"What'd you expect?" Washington asked, perplexed. "Something different? What'd you want it to do, sound better when you slammed it? Doors don't play favorites, Mr. Kotter. They don't know who's slamming them."

Julie came in from the kitchen with a tray of soft drinks and sandwiches. "Hi!" she said to Kotter. "Want an appetizer before dinner?"

"I don't know. What are we having for dinner?"

"The appetizer," she told him. "I haven't had time to prepare anything else. I'm proofreading the copy for the next edition of the *Sweathog*." She put the tray down and headed back toward the kitchen. "Eat hearty!"

Kotter sank into a chair.

"You can't stay there," Barbarino said to him. "I was just going to tell everybody about the deal that Mr. Woodman offered me today. He doesn't want you to know about it yet. He wants it to be a surprise."

"*Woodman* offered you a deal?" Washington said dubiously.

"All of us," Barbarino replied. "He wants to put us in charge of the *Booster*."

"In *complete* charge?" Kotter asked.

"Mr. Kotter, you're not supposed to know about this."

"In *complete* charge?" Epstein asked.

"Right. In complete charge—under his guidance," Barbarino said. "But, here's the deal: When we graduate—if ever—he'll write us a glowing letter of recommendation. And with that glowing letter of recommendation we can walk into the office of any big city newspaper in the country."

"And then what?" Kotter asked.

"Mr. Kotter, you're not supposed to know about this," Barbarino said again.

"What's a glowing letter of recommendation?" Epstein asked.

"That's a letter that Mr. Woodman writes about how good you are—then he sets fire to it," Horshack said. "Hahh . . . hahh . . . hahh . . . hahh . . ."

"I don't think I'm going to need anything like that," Washington said. "This deal I got offered to me today is going to give me everything I'll ever need." He then told the others about his meeting in the alley with the coach from Darby Academy.

"Would you be rich, too, if you went to that school?" Barbarino asked him.

"I don't know about that," Washington said, "but at least I'd have a chance of getting *out* of school. What it takes is good grades. I don't see how I'm ever going to make it where I am now." He turned to Epstein. "What's your deal?"

Epstein told them about his conversation with the owner of the drugstore, McNary.

"A whole year's advertising!" Washington said enthusiastically when Epstein finished. "With that in our pocket, we could really start making some money with this paper!"

"Mr. Kotter, what do you think we ought to do?" Horshack said.

"I can't *tell* you what to do, that will have to be your own decision," he replied. "I think you ought to realize, though, that you're facing your first test of ethics with your paper."

"Mr. Kotter, you're not in school now, forget about tests," Washington said.

"Furthermore," Kotter continued, "you've brought the situation on yourselves. Your paper has stories in it about things that never really happened."

"You can't prove that," Epstein said. "We didn't use any names."

"And all the storekeepers had to do to get stories on their stores in the paper was buy advertising," Kotter went on. "You as much as announced that you were for sale, that you and your paper could be bought. So, is it any wonder that now you're being offered bribes?"

"We're not wondering how it happened, we're wondering what to do about it," Barbarino said.

"As I said before—that's *your* decision to make."

"Mr. Kotter is right," Washington said. "This is all wrong. That coach coming to me and offering me a scholarship and good grades and all that for some publicity. And McNary wanting a story from Epstein to run down his competition. And Mr. Woodman telling Barbarino he'd put us in charge of the *Booster*. It's wrong! Wrong!"

"What's wrong about it?" Epstein asked puzzledly.

"Don't you see, man?" Washington replied. "The *Sweathog*, it doesn't just belong to me or you or Barbarino. We all started it together. You and me and Barbarino and Horshack and Vernajean and Rosalie. It belongs to all of us. It wouldn't be fair for some of us to cash in and the others to end up with zero."

"Yeah—I see!" Epstein said.

"What we'll do," Washington said, "is wait until Horshack and Rosalie and Vernajean gets some offers made to them, too, then we'll *all* cash in!"

"I'll drink to that," Horshack said, picking up a soft drink from the tray.

"Mr. Kotter, thanks," Washington said. "We're sure lucky we got you to straighten us out."

Kotter got up and trudged wearily toward the kitchen.

SEVEN

The sweathogs were only half-awake as they trudged through the morning dimness on their way to pick up the new edition of the paper.

"Who decided the *Sweathog* was going to be a morning paper?" Barbarino complained. "What's the matter with a night paper? I'm at my best at night. I never have any trouble keeping my eyes open when I'm watching the late show—or the *late* late show. But when the sun comes up, man, all I want to do it sleep."

"That's interesting," Epstein said to him. "I never guessed before that you were normal."

"Nobody would buy a night paper," Washington said. "People want their bad news in the morning. That way, they can worry about it at work. They don't want to worry about it at night and ruin the late show—and the *late* late show."

When they reached the print shop a short while later, they found Happy Harrison, the printer, waiting for them in his office. Happy did not look happy.

"What's happened?" Washington said. "Where are the papers?"

"The papers are ready," Happy Harrison replied. "They're printed—the usual beautiful job—and waiting."

"I don't see them. Where are they?"

"They're hiding," Happy Harrison told him. "The last word I had was that they won't come out until the party of the first part—that's you—and the party of the second part—that's me—finish up with a little unfinished business."

"What're you talking about? What business?" Washington said. "We got a deal."

Harrison nodded. "That's what I said to my printers when they told me they wanted a raise," he said. "'What raise?' I asked them. 'We got a deal,' I said. You know what they told me? They told me they were all going to come down with brain concussions. If they did that, who'd run the presses? So, to keep them healthy, I gave them a raise."

"What's that got to do with us?" Epstein asked.

"When I was a young man, I got some very good advice from my father," Happy Harrison said. "When things go bad, he told me, don't just sit around and mope—pass it on to somebody else. That's what I'm doing. What it costs me to give my printers a raise, I'm passing on to my customers."

"Man, we can't pay you any more," Washington said. "You're already getting all the money we make on advertising."

"Is that all?" Harrison said, surprised. "Don't I get a share of what you sell the papers for? How did I make a deal like that? The softness in my heart must be going to my head in my middle-age."

"If we give you any *more* money, we won't make any profit," Epstein said.

"That's what I told my printers. 'If I give you a raise, I can't make a profit,' I said. Right away they started getting headaches from the brain concussions they had coming on." He put his hands to his forehead. "I'm getting it myself," he said sorrowfully. "The throbbing . . . the throbbing . . ."

"Okay, okay, how *much* more money do you want?" Washington asked.

"Well, let's see. . . . I thought I was already getting half of what you were getting for selling the papers. So, if I asked for that, I wouldn't be gaining anything, I'd only be getting even. So, I've got to have half of the half that was left over when I thought I was already getting half."

"We got to have a conference," Washington told him.

"Don't keep me waiting too long," Happy Harrison said. "It causes tension. Tension makes the headache worse. A headache can turn into a brain concussion just like—" he snapped his fingers, "—that."

The sweathogs left the office, stepping out into the anteroom.

"What kind of change is that guy talking about?" Washington asked the others. "What's a half of a half that was left over when he thought he was already getting half?"

"It's some kind of math, I think," Barbarino said. "Trigonography or calculationus or something."

"I think we're supposed to bargain with him,"

Horshack said. "When he tells us he wants half of the half that was left over when he thought he was already getting half, we're supposed to offer him half of that."

Happy Harrison sang out from inside the office. "Throbbing . . . throbbing . . . throbbing . . ."

"We got to go back in there," Washington said. "But what do we tell him?"

"Maybe he's bluffing," Epstein said. "Let's say 'no' and see what happens."

The others agreed.

"We thought it over," Washington told Happy Harrison, as the sweathogs rejoined him in his office. "And the answer is no."

Harrison began putting on his coat.

"Where you going?" Washington asked, puzzled.

"I'm checking into a hospital with my brain concussion."

"Hold it! What about our papers?"

"Papers? Papers? I don't understand a word you're saying," Happy Harrison replied. "I'm in worse condition than I thought. I think I've got Asian brain concussion."

"Okay, okay, man," Washington said, surrendering. "Give us our papers and you get your half."

"And also my half of the other half?"

"Whatever," Washington replied.

Harrison beamed. "I'm cured!" he said. He began getting out of his coat. "It's a miracle!"

"How are we going to know how much of the money we make is ours?" Barbarino asked, as the sweathogs approached the school with the bundles of papers under their arms."

"Easy," Epstein said. "We give everything to Happy Harrison and what he gives us back belongs to us."

"I got a feeling the only thing Happy Harrison is gonna give anybody is the Asian brain concussion," Washington said.

"He bombed us," Epstein agreed. "But what can we do about it?"

"We can take that advice that Happy Harrison's father gave him," Horshack said. "Things are going bad for us, so let's pass it on."

"How?"

"Raise prices," Horshack said.

"Yeah, that's only right," Washington said. "Do unto others as others have done unto you."

At the main entrance to the school they separated. Washington, Barbarino and Epstein went inside to peddle their papers in the corridors and Horshack remained at the main door.

"Paper! Paper!" Horshack began chanting. "Get your *Sweathog* now before the price goes up again!"

The students who were arriving at school passed him by without even glancing at him.

"Read all about it!" Horshack shouted. "Human tragedy! Crime! S-e-x!"

Still there were no buyers.

"Corruption continues in school system!" Horshack cried out. "Read about the big paper clip heist!"

At last, a customer—one of the hoods who had invaded the newspaper office a few days earlier.

"Lousy Louie sent me," the hood said. "He wants me to get a paper and read it to me."

"The price has gone up," Horshack said, handing him a paper.

"How much?"

"It's double," Horshack said.

The hood shrugged. "I didn't pay for the last paper I got," he said, departing, "so I guess double that won't break me."

"I hope that's the copy that has the Asian brain concussion germs on it!" Horshack called after him. Then he began hawking the *Sweathog* again. "Read all about it! Hike in subway fare ends love affair!"

The students continued to stream by, however, untempted by the paper that he was now brandishing anxiously.

"Sale!" Horshack bellowed. "All papers half-price!"

Not even that incentive drew a buyer.

A few moments later, Washington, Barbarino and Epstein returned. They appeared to be carrying as many papers under their arms as when they had entered the school.

"We can't sell none," Barbarino told Horshack.

"You either? Thank God!" Horshack said. "I thought it was me!"

"How come, all of a sudden, the *Sweathog* is selling like arm pits?" Washington asked the others. "Is it the price?"

"It must be the price," Epstein said.

"I don't think it's the price," Horshack said. "I *cut* the price. It didn't help."

"You didn't cut it enough, that's all," Washington said. "Watch this." He began waving a paper. "Get your *Sweathog*!" he shouted. "Last chance! Read all about it! Human tragedy! Crime! Get your *free* copy right here! All copies of the *Sweathog* free today, folks! Don't push—form an orderly line! Yo! Yo! Yo!

It's freeby day! Get your *Sweathog!* Get it *free!* I said *free,* folks! Not a dime! Not a quarter! Today and today only, the *Sweathog* is selling for the tenth part of nothing! Free! Free! Free!"

He had attracted not one customer.

"We can't even give it away," Barbarino said dismally.

"Who says!" Washington snapped. He grabbed a student who was passing by and shoved a paper under the student's arm. "You take that, man," he warned, "or it's you and me after school, bare knuckles!"

Clutching the paper fearfully, the student hurried on.

"Okay, that's one gone," Washington said. "All we needed was the right gimmick. We got to use force."

"That's all right for you," Horshack said. "But what about me? I'll have to pay them to take the papers."

"We're not going to make any money that way," Epstein pointed out.

"And poor Happy Harrison," Horshack said. "He's the big loser."

"It don't make sense," Washington said. "Last time, we could have sold twice as many papers. This time, we can't sell any. What happened?"

"Somebody ought to ask somebody who's not buying," Horshack suggested.

"You ask," Epstein said.

"People lie to me," Horshack said. "Washington better do the asking."

Washington grabbed another student, this time a girl. "I got a question," he told her.

"The answer is yes!" she said delightedly.

"Yes what?"

"Yes, I'll be your fox," she said.

"That's not the question," Washington told her. "The question is: how come you didn't buy a *Sweathog?*"

She looked at the sweathogs. "I didn't know they was for sale," she replied. "But, anyway, what do I want with any of them when I got you?"

"You haven't got me, woman. I'm taking a survey. The question was about the *Sweathog* the paper, not the sweathog the sweathogs. How come you didn't buy a paper?"

"I got fooled once on that paper," she said. "You gave me all that stuff about that tragedy and crime and sex, but you didn't tell me who done it. It's no fun talking about what. All the fun is in talking about who."

"You could guess who, couldn't you?" Washington argued.

"I don't need a paper to guess about people," she said. "What I bought the paper for was so I'd *know*. You tell me who's who," she said, moving on, "and I'll buy your paper again."

"That's what Mr. Kotter said," Horshack reminded the others, "people want to know who."

"That's only one teacher's and one fox's opinion," Washington said. "For a survey to be any good, you got to talk to a *lot* of people—three, four, five, six." He grabbed another student, a boy. "You don't care if the *Sweathog's* got names in it or not, do you?" he said.

The boy looked at him warily. "Is that an order or just a hint?" he asked.

"It's neither, man. All I want in the truth."

"Maybe it's because it hasn't got any names in it,"

the boy said. "But if you want some other truth, it's okay with me. Just tell me what you want."

Washington released him, sending him on his way.

"Okay, that's two that want names—Mr. Kotter and that fox—and one undecided," he said. He grabbed another student, a girl again.

"How come you didn't buy a *Sweathog?*" he asked.

She stomped on his foot. "Don't you grab me, you male chauvinist pig!" she said. She strode on.

"Two for names, one undecided, and one 'don't know.'" Washington said.

The bell rang.

"Names wins, two to two," Barbarino said, as they headed for the classroom.

"That's a tie," Washington said. "We got to survey some more. Because if names wins that means we got to go out and dig up some real stories about real people. We can't just sit around making up stories any more. You know what that is, don't you?"

"That's work," Barbarino said glumly.

"So, what do we do?" Washington said.

"Keep surveying—until it comes out right," Horshack said.

"And don't tell Mr. Kotter we didn't sell any *Sweathogs* today," Washington said.

"Won't he guess when he sees us carrying all these papers?" Epstein said.

"We'll tell him these are for the files," Washington said.

Julie was waiting for the sweathogs with a tray of soft drinks and iced cupcakes when they arrived at the newspaper office that afternoon.

"You're late," she said.

"We been finishing up a survey," Epstein told her.

Julie noticed that Washington was limping. "What happened?" she asked.

"Man, this womens' lib movement is getting out of hand," he said. "You ask a simple question and you get stomped on."

The sweathogs dumped their unsold papers in a corner, then dropped into chairs.

"Those papers . . ." Julie said.

"That corner over there, that's the file cabinet," Washington said.

"Oh. What was the survey about?"

"About two stomps too long," Washington said. "We should have stopped when it was a tie."

"We learned, sort of, that the readers might like to see some names in the *Sweathog*," Horshack told Julie.

"How 'sort of?' " she asked.

"Ten to two," Horshack replied.

"We surveyed the wrong readers," Washington said crossly. "What do feet-stompers know about what they want to read in a paper!"

"If you want my opinion . . ." Julie began.

Washington quickly pulled back his feet.

"No, not that," she said. "It's my opinion . . ."

The apartment door was opening.

"Gabe . . ." Julie said.

It was not Kotter who appeared, however. It was Lousy Louie's two hoods. They entered and closed the door, then stood glowering ominously at the sweathogs. One of the hoods had a copy of the *Sweathog*.

"You can't just walk into an apartment like that!" Julie said indignantly.

"How else is dere, lady?" one of the hoods asked.

"You're supposed to ring or knock."

"Knock, knock," the second hood said. "Okay—you satisfied?"

The first hood spoke again. "You done it again," he said to the sweathogs. "Didn't I tell you? No more stories on Lousy Louie."

"There's no story on Lousy Louie in there," Washington said.

"Lousy Louie says dere is. And when Lousy Louie says dere is, dere is." He opened the paper. "Right here. Dis story about da outfit dat's printing up counterfeit baseball cards. Dat's Lousy Louie."

"That's a made-up story!" Epstein said.

"Yeah? How come da story says da counterfeit baseball cards has got Tom Seaver playing first base for the Toledo Mudhens? Dat happens to be—by no mere co-incidence—da same little mistake dat appears among Lousy Louie's counterfeit baseball cards."

"That's the kind of mistake *anybody* could make," Washington said. "Lousy Louie isn't the *only* dummy in the world."

"Sure, it's a natural," Horshack said to the hood. "You put a guy in California making up counterfeit baseball cards and another guy in Florida making up counterfeit baseball cards, and the chances are probably a hundred-to-one that they'll both have Tom Seaver playing first base for the Toledo Mudhens."

The first hood turned to the second hood. "Whatta you think, Vincent? Could dat happen?"

"Anything is possible," the second hood replied. "Remember da time we dumped da body in da ocean, twenty miles out to sea, and it came up in da guy's swimming pool in Hoboken?"

The first hood faced the sweathogs again. "Okay, dis time we don't dump youse in da river," he said.

"There goes my chance to visit Hoboken," Horshack said.

"But we got to do something to you dat we can tell Lousy Louie," the hood said. He looked around. "Did you get a new typewriter?"

"We use pencils," Washington said.

The first hood addressed the second hood again. "Vincent . . ."

The second hood began breaking the pencils in two.

"Dat don't seem enough," the first hood said. "It won't satisfy Lousy Louie." He pointed to the tray of soft drinks and iced cupcakes. "Over dere next, Vincent," he said.

Finished with the pencils, the second hood began breaking the cupcakes in two.

"We will now take our leavings," the first hood said, opening the door. "But, remember, any more stories on Lousy Louie and—one way or anudder—youse are gonna end up in Hoboken."

The door closed behind them.

Julie snatched up the tray. "Maybe I can save the cupcakes!" she said anxiously, hurrying toward the kitchen. "I'll try glueing them back together with icing."

The apartment door opened again. This time it was Kotter who entered.

"Wasn't that Lousy Louie's hoods I just saw in the hall?" he said to the sweathogs.

"Louie thought he was in the *Sweathog* again,"

Washington said. "The story on the counterfeit base-ball cards."

"Was he right?"

"It was just chance," Washington replied.

"Sure," Horshack said, "you put one guy in California making up counterfeit baseball cards and another guy in Florida . . ."

"Don't say all that again," Washington said. "We got a bigger problem than Lousy Louie."

"Yes, I see," Kotter said, looking toward the corner where the unsold papers were stacked. "If you publish a few more editions of the *Sweathog*, you'll have to take over somebody else's apartment just to hold your files."

"Mr. Kotter, you're right," Epstein said. "We took a survey. The readers told us the same thing you told us, we got to have names."

"As a matter of fact, if you don't start using names, you better stop carrying crime stories," Kotter said. "Because I don't think there's any crime story that you can write that Lousy Louie won't think it's about him. And with good reason. Apparently he has a monopoly on crime in this neighborhood."

"Not yet," Horshack said. "There's still the paper clip story."

"Yeah, maybe we could build that up—make another Watergate out of it," Washington said.

"And Lousy Louie would muscle in on it and you'd be right back where you started," Kotter said.

"We got no choice," Barbarino said. "The worst has finally come to the worst. We got to start running some real stories about real people with real names."

"Sure, we can make up some real names," Horshack said.

"Let's get at it," Washington said, rising and heading for the door. "We got a whole paper to fill. We need names, names, names."

"I know a guy at Attica," Barbarino said, as the other sweathogs trailed after Washington. "We could use his name. He goes by a number these days."

"But we got to have a story to go along with it," Washington said, opening the door and leading the way out.

"He's got a story," Barbarino said. "I didn't believe it until recently. But now I think maybe he was telling the truth. He claims he was dumped in the ocean, twenty miles out to sea, and came up in a swimming . . ."

Kotter missed the end of the story, as Horshack, the last sweathog out, slammed the door behind him.

Smiling optimistically, Kotter went into the kitchen, where he found Julie pinning cupcake halves together with toothpicks.

"Hi!" Julie said. "I thought I heard your voice out there. But I couldn't leave my cupcakes." She looked at him closely. "Has something good happened?"

"The *Sweathog* is about to become defunct," he told her.

"That's terrible!"

"Our guests, the newspaper people, will be moving out."

"That's nice. What makes you so sure?"

"The public has discovered that the *Sweathog* is a rip-off," Kotter told her. "The public has stopped buying. So, the sweathogs have set out to dig up some real stories about real people with real names."

"Well . . . won't that save the paper?"

"It might—if they actually did it," Kotter said. "But coming up with real stories about real people with real names takes work. I don't think the sweathogs are that interested in newspapering. Their goal, all along, has been to put the *Booster* out of business, not to put out an honest, relevant, worthwhile paper."

"Mmmmm . . . I see what you mean. Well . . . so long *Sweathog*."

"And hello privacy," Kotter said. He frowned suddenly. "Is that voodoo?" he asked, as Julie plunged another toothpick into a cupcake.

"Pardon?"

"The way witch doctors stick pins in dolls," Kotter explained.

"No," she said, shaking her head. "These toothpicks are just to hold them together until the glue dries. Although . . ." she said, looking thoughtful.

"What?"

"Well . . . I mean, I don't believe in that hocus-pocus, voodoo. But, just suppose . . ." She pointed to one of the cupcakes. "Just suppose I named that one Lousy Louie. Would anything happen, do you think?"

"Not a chance."

"You're right. Besides, it would be childish."

"We have to leave it to the law to handle people like Lousy Louie," Kotter said.

Julie picked up the icing gun. "Still . . ." she said.

"You print his name on the cupcake," Kotter said, going toward the cupboard, "and I'll get more toothpicks."

EIGHT

When Kotter entered the kitchen for breakfast he found not the usual two newspapers—his and the neighbor's—but three. The third was the new edition of the *Sweathog*. He also found his wife in a mild state of shock. Her eyes were glazed and she was having trouble functioning. Proof of the latter was that she was breaking an egg into her mug of coffee.

"Do you save time that way, drinking your egg with your coffee?" he asked. "Does the toast go in there too?"

"Oh, no!" Julie said, seeing what she had done. "That egg was supposed to be for you. I wonder if I can save it?"

"No chance," Kotter said. "It's a scientific fact that eggs cannot breathe under coffee. That's a drowned egg."

"It's the paper's fault," Julie said. "It's got me so shook up, I don't know what I'm doing. Look!" she said, pointing to the *Sweathog*. "They did it! They actually did it!"

Kotter picked up the paper and read the headline:

SWEATHOG EXPOSES MR. BIG
OF INTERNATIONAL CRIME

Kotter sat down, shaken. "It can't be," he said. "What's the gimmick?"

"No gimmick," Julie told him. "It's true. They have his name and they have the facts. Read," she said.

Sipping coffee, Kotter read the entire story. "You're right," he said when he finished. "It's all here. The name—Hugo Jonas. And the facts—the million dollar bank robbery in London, the drug operation in Paris, the car theft ring in Los Angeles, the art forgery operation in Rome—it's all here." He put the paper down. "Fantastic."

"Now do you see why I was so shook up?"

"Well, it's startling, yes," Kotter conceded, "but no reason to go ape—not when you have an egg in your hand."

"Then how come you're *drinking* that egg?" Julie asked.

Kotter pushed the coffee mug away. "I was destroying the evidence," he said. "There's a stiff rap in this state for drowning an egg."

"Gabe, how did they do it?" Julie said. "The Mr. Big of international crime! And they have all the facts! How did they *do* it?"

"Luck," Kotter replied. "It had to be luck. They must have found the information written on a wall with spray paint. I think that's all they read. That or . . ."

"Or what?"

"Well, how do you know that all these facts are true?" Kotter said. "Maybe there was a million dollar bank robbery in London, but maybe there wasn't. I don't know—do you?"

Julie shook her head. "But they have Mr. Big's name—Hugo Jonas," she said. "If he *isn't* Mr. Big, how could they use his name?"

"Maybe they made up the name, too," Kotter said.

"I don't think so. Hugo Jonas *sounds* like Mr. Big's name."

"I still think there's something fishy about the whole thing," Kotter said, picking up the paper again. "There are no names used in these other stories," he said, reading.

"Who cares about the other stories?" Julie said. "When you've named the Mr. Big of international crime, you've done enough name naming for one edition."

"Here's an interesting paragraph," Kotter said. "It seems that the nation's biggest fence has checked into a hospital."

"Oh, no! Gabe, what have we done? What is he in the hospital for?"

"It's minor. He stepped on something in his bare feet and he's having it removed."

"Not . . ."

Kotter nodded. "A toothpick."

When Kotter arrived at the school, Horshack was at the main entrance, hawking the *Sweathog* and selling copies to the arriving students as fast as he could hand them out and collect for them. Kotter stopped for a moment to watch.

"Get your *Sweathog!*" Horshack was crying. "Mr. Big exposed! Read all about it! Who masterminded the million-dollar London bank robbery? Who heads the Paris drug ring? Who do you see in L.A. for a deal on a stolen car? Why is that Mona Lisa you bought in Rome smirking? Read all about it! Get your *Sweathog!*"

Kotter moved on, entering the school and heading for his classroom. A few seconds later he heard his name called. Turning, he saw Charley Piper hurrying after him. Piper was clutching a copy of the *Sweathog.*

"Don't believe everything you read in the papers," Kotter said, as Piper caught up to him.

"But it's right here, the name, the dates, the crimes," Piper said.

"The mysterious subway lovers were there, too," Kotter replied, as they walked on. "But you don't believe they ever really existed, do you?"

Piper's face fell. "They didn't? You mean I've been wasting my time looking for Miss Wrong on the subway?"

"Miss Wrong?"

"That's how I think of her," Piper said. "I'm not interested in anything permanent, just one mad moment of ecstacy between stops."

"You have about as much chance of meeting Miss Wrong on the subway as the sweathogs have of coming up with the name of the Mr. Big of international crime," Kotter said, as they reached the door to his classroom and halted. "Think!" he said. "Where would they get information like that?"

"Maybe they found a confession in a bottle that washed up on the beach at Coney Island."

"A bottle would never make it to the beach," Kotter said. "The pollution is too thick."

"Maybe it was a submarine bottle and it came in *under* the pollution."

"Charley, admit it—you don't believe that Mr. Big story either, do you?"

"Not *all* of it, no," Piper replied. "I don't think Mr. Big really got a million bucks in that London heist. It probably wasn't any more than nine-hundred-and-ninety-nine thousand. They always use round figures when they announce those robberies. Oh-oh," he said suddenly, looking past Kotter, "here comes the Mr. Big of the paper clip racket!"

Kotter saw the assistant principal approaching from the far end of the corridor.

"Why does he look happy?" Piper said.

"Some terrible tragedy somewhere, I suppose," Kotter said.

"Have you seen the *Sweathog!*" Woodman said, nearing them. "My confidence in those lads has paid off. It's the story of the year! Of the decade! Of the century! We'll win the Pulitzer Prize!"

"We?" Kotter said.

"Well, I feel partly responsible for it," Woodman said. "They couldn't have done it if I hadn't encouraged them. I knew they had the stuff in them. I've known it all along. Oh, true, I've appeared to be disapproving at times. But that's my technique. It spurs the young people to work hard and sacrifice to prove to me that I'm wrong about them. That's the secret to success—hard work and sacrifice."

"Are we still talking about the sweathogs?" Kotter asked.

"I taught them everything they know about newspapering," Woodman went on. "I did it by example. They got their training for the Pulitzer Prize by reading the *Booster*."

"A lot can be learned from bad example," Kotter agreed.

"I'll probably be hearing from the newspapers soon—the real newspapers, that is," Woodman said. "They'll want pictures of me—with the sweathogs, of course. I expect they'll want to do a story on me, too—how I took those kids under my wing and turned them into pros."

"You've been busy," Charley Piper said. "How did you find time for the paper clip rip-off?"

Woodman glared at him. "Aren't you supposed to be in your classroom, Piper?"

"See you, Gabe," Piper said, departing. "I just remembered I'm supposed to be in my classroom."

"When the papers call me," Woodman said to Kotter when Piper had gone, "they'll undoubtedly want to know how the sweathogs dug up that marvelous story on Mr. Big. I can guess how it was done, of course. But, just for the record, what was the sweathogs' *modus operandi*?"

"They just walked along the beach until a bottle surfaced," Kotter said. "Then a hatch opened and this little man handed them Mr. Big's confession."

Woodman chuckled grimly. "That's not funny, Kotter. I mean business."

"I don't know how they got the story."

"You *do* know!" Woodman said sharply. "Those scalawags tell you everything!"

"Scalawags!" Kotter said. "Winning the Pulitzer has

done a lot for the sweathogs. The last time we talked, you called them hoodlums."

"Stop that beating around the bush!" Woodman said, getting a paper clip from his pocket. "Where did they get that story?"

"I honestly don't know," Kotter said. "But I have an idea."

"Yes?" Woodman asked eagerly, straightening the paper clip.

"I've told this to only one other person," Kotter said, speaking secretively.

"Who?"

"My wife."

"That hush-hush, is it?" Woodman said, impressed. "I feel privileged, Kotter. I also assure you that the secret is safe with me. Now ... how did they get that story?"

"I think they made it up," Kotter told him.

Woodman snorted angrily. "You're lying! You and those hoodlums want to keep all the glory for yourselves!"

"I swear on a stack of social studies text books—I think they made it up," Kotter said.

"Impossible! They have Mr. Big's name—Hugo Jonas! And they have the facts—dates, times, places!"

"All made up—I think."

"Kotter, I have it in my power to make things very unpleasant for you at this school!" Woodman warned.

Kotter shook his head. "I anticipated that," he said. "You won't get *my* paper clips. I take them home with me every night after classes and lock them up."

Woodman exploded in a gusher of irate sounds, then stomped off.

As Kotter entered his classroom, the second bell rang. A few moments later, the sweathogs arrived. They were buoyant, congratulating themselves on their new success.

"We sold out again, Mr. Kotter!" Horshack said.

"Man, at this rate, Happy Harrison is gonna be the richest printer in Brooklyn!" Washington said.

"Well, don't count Harrison's chickens before you hatch them," Kotter said. "You may not be able to come up with another big scoop for the next issue."

"We can do it," Washington said confidently.

"Interesting story—the Mr. Big of international crime," Kotter said. "How did you get it?"

Silence.

"Maybe you got it from some anonymous tipster," Kotter suggested.

"Mr. Kotter, we can't tell you," Barbarino said. "We got to protect our source."

"Yeah, that's the journalistic code," Washington said. "If we don't protect our sources, all the sources will take their business to the other papers."

"Uh-huh," Kotter said. "Let me ask this. Is there a real Hugo Jonas?"

"Yeah, man," Washington replied. "Didn't you read the story? He's the Mr. Big of international crime."

"You can look him up in the international telephone book," Horshack said.

Kotter was still not convinced. "This Hugo Jonas is actually a real person?"

"We even watched him at work," Barbarino said. "He really cleans up."

"Knock it off!" Washington said. "We got to protect our source."

"If he's the international Mr. Big, what was he doing here in this neighborhood?" Kotter asked.

"On a job," Barbarino replied. "I told you he was cleaning up."

"Man," Washington complained to Barbarino, "you are going to give away our source."

"All right," Kotter said, "I won't ask any more. But I still find it hard to believe ..." He interrupted himself, looking out the window. "What's the FBI doing here, I wonder," he said. "We don't have a course in violating civil rights, do we?"

"What FBI?" Washington said.

"Six men just got out of a car and they're walking toward the school," Kotter said, still looking out the window.

"How do you know they're FBI?"

"They're all wearing blue serge suits."

Behind Kotter there was a sudden sound of wild scrambling. As he turned to find out what was happening he saw the last of the sweathogs, Horshack, disappear through the door.

"Come back!" Kotter called. "I could be wrong! Maybe they're blue serge suit salesmen!"

There was no reply.

Kotter went to the door and looked out into the corridor. The sweathogs were nowhere in sight. He shrugged, puzzled, then returned to the windows. A second later, he saw the sweathogs leave the school, running. Horshack was still bringing up the rear.

"I wonder if it was something I said?" Kotter asked himself.

As he was walking back toward his desk, the assistant principal came hustling into the room. He was accompanied by six men in blue serge suits.

"Where are your students?" Woodman asked gruffly.

"I don't get students until my next class," Kotter replied. "I have the sweathogs for this class."

"That's who I'm talking about!" Woodman said. "Where are they?"

Kotter hesitated for a second. "It's very possible that they're on a field trip," he said. "Or maybe it's track and field I'm thinking of. I know there's a lot of running involved."

"Kotter, you're not making any sense."

One of the men in the blue serge suits stepped forward. "Smith—FBI," he said. He opened the copy of the *Sweathog* he was carrying to the story on Mr. Big. "What do you know about this?" he asked.

"Aren't you going to introduce me to your friends?" Kotter replied.

"We're *all* Smith," Smith told him.

"I see—the names came with the suits."

"Kotter, answer the man's questions!" Woodman commanded.

"Oh—the story," Kotter said. "Well, I thought it was a little short on punctuation. All the capitals seemed to be there, though—not always in the right place, but there. That's an improvement. At one time, the sweathogs would only capitalize verbs."

"Stop trying to protect those hoodlums!" Woodman said.

"What have they done?" Kotter asked Smith. "It isn't against the law for a newspaper to run a crime story."

"We don't want your students, we want Hugo

Jonas," Smith replied. "Your students know where he is."

"Well, *I* don't know where he is. And I don't know where the sweathogs are, either," Kotter said. "And, as long as I'm telling you everything I don't know, you might as well know that I don't even know that there *is* a Hugo Jonas. I think that story is pure fiction."

"What about the facts?" Smith said.

"If they made up Hugo Jonas, they could also make up the facts."

Smith rattled the paper. "They didn't make up *these* facts," he told Kotter. "We've checked out every detail in this story and it's all true."

"It couldn't be."

"It is. We ran the story through the computer," Smith said.

"Every month, I get a bill from a department store in Cincinnati," Kotter countered. "A computer does *that* too!"

"Why don't you pay the bill?"

"I've never *been* to Cincinnati."

Smith turned to a second Smith. "Check that out," he said. "He claims he's never been to Cincinnati."

"Check it out how?" the second Smith asked.

"Run it through the computer."

"I've never been to Detroit, either," Kotter said to the second Smith. "You can put that in your computer, too."

"What was your name before you changed it to Hugo Jonas?" the first Smith asked Kotter suddenly.

Kotter smiled. "Tricky, tricky," he said. "But you've got the wrong Mr. Big. Everywhere but in the classroom and at home, I'm known as Shorty."

Smith eyed him narrowly. "We'll find those students," he said menacingly.

"If you do, tell them Shorty says 'Hi.'"

The Smiths turned sharply and marched out. Woodman hurried after them.

"Everybody keeps running out on me today," Kotter said. "Is it me? Is it . . ." He suddenly brightened. "Of course—that's it! I'm on the sixth day of my five-day deodorant!"

When Kotter entered the apartment that afternoon after school he was struck by a sudden blinding light.

"Julie!" he cried out, shielding his eyes with his arms. "What happened?"

She came rushing in from the kitchen. "It's all right!" she told him. "We had the windows washed today!"

Slowly, carefully, Kotter lowered his arms. "Why?" he asked. "We've *never* had the windows washed before. Our landlord thinks dirty windows are next to godliness. What changed his mind?"

"I don't know. All I know is, all of a sudden, there was the window washer, standing on the ledge outside the windows, washing."

"Clean windows!" Kotter said rapturously. He sighed. "Unfortunately, I can't stay and enjoy them."

"Why not?"

"I have to go out and look for the sweathogs," he told her. He looked at the windows again. "This is probably the last time I'll ever see them this way. Tomorrow, they'll be dirty again."

"Look for the sweathogs why?"

Kotter told her about the visit by the FBI men. "Evidently, I was wrong," he said. "The sweathogs didn't make up that story. There is a Hugo Jonas. And he's the Mr. Big of international crime. And, somehow, the sweathogs know where he is."

"Why don't you let the FBI find them?" Julie said. "All they want to do is ask them questions."

"I'm not worried about what the FBI might do. I'm thinking about Mr. Big."

"Oh, my!" Julie said. "I didn't think about that."

"You know what almost happened when Lousy Louie only *thought* there was a story about him in the Sweathog. If Mr. Big is as big as the sweathogs' story claims, he probably has his mr. littles out looking for them."

"Even if Mr. Big is only medium-size, I wouldn't want to be in the sweathogs' shoes right now," Julie agreed. She headed for the closet. "Let me get my coat," she said. "I'll go with you."

"No," Kotter said, stopping her. "Somebody has to be here in case the sweathogs show up. Stay here and think of some place to hide them."

"Hide them? Here? With our windows washed? This is practically like living outdoors."

"Mix up some grime and throw it on the windows," Kotter suggested, going to the apartment door.

"All right. But it's such a shame. That window washer did such a good job. He was so conscientious. He spent *hours* on our windows. He—Gabe! That's explains it!"

Kotter halted at the door. "Explains what?"

"Well, I thought it was sort of odd. Usually, they wear coveralls. I was just thinking . . . about the FBI . . . and I suddenly realized."

"Yes? What?"

"The window washer. He had on a blue serge suit."

"Oh ... I forgot to mention that," Kotter said. "They think I'm Mr. Big."

"What ever gave them *that* idea, for heaven's sake?"

"They're not sure. At this point, it's just a suspicion. It's my fault. I shouldn't have mentioned that bill we get every month from that department store in Cincinnati."

"Gabe, you're not making any sense."

"If you think it's confusing now, wait'll we start getting a bill from a department store in Detroit," Kotter said. "I know that's what's going to happen. Because the FBI is going to run me through its computer and during our conversation I happened to mention Detroit."

"What will I do if the FBI men come here while you're gone?" Julie asked.

Kotter thought a moment. "Just stash that haul from the London bank job and wipe that smirk off the Mona Lisa's face," he said, going out.

"When will you be back?"

"Thirty years to life," he answered. "Or, with time off for good behavior, maybe an hour or so."

The door closed.

NINE

When Kotter had been gone almost three hours, Julie began to be more than a little concerned about him. She kept watch at the windows, but since it was now dark out, the only thing she could see clearly was that the windows were already fogging up with grime again. Then at last the doorbell rang.

"Who is it?" Julie called out apprehensively, going to the door.

"It's me, Gabe. The door is locked."

"I locked it to keep the FBI out—or to keep Mr. Big out, whichever came first."

"Good idea," Kotter said. "Now, let me in."

"How do I know it's you?"

"Don't you recognize my voice?"

"Maybe you're the FBI or Mr. Big doing an imitation."

"Julie, it's me," Kotter said wearily. "I've been

trudging around the neighborhood for three hours. Let me in."

"If you're who you say you are," she said, "why don't you use your key?"

"I don't have my key. I must have left it in another pair of trousers or in the bedroom or somewhere."

"A likely story!" Julie said. "That's exactly what the FBI or Mr. Big would say."

"You want me to *prove* who I am?" Kotter said. "I'll describe myself. Tall, handsome, mustache, dark hair."

"That describes your tall, handsome, dark mustache, now what about the rest of you?"

"Wicked twinkle in the eye."

"How are you dressed?"

"Shoes, socks, shorts, shirt, trousers, sports jacket . . ."

"That sounds like you," Julie conceded. "One more thing: what are you holding in your right hand?"

"Nothing."

"Gabe—it's you!" Julie cried out happily, unlocking the door and throwing it open wide.

Kotter stood in the hallway. "What convinced you?" he asked.

"Well, you weren't wearing a blue serge suit, so I knew you weren't the FBI. And your right hand was empty, so you couldn't be Mr. Big."

Kotter pondered for a second. "The reasoning escapes me," he said.

"I picture Mr. Big standing at a gaming table at Monte Carlo," Julie explained. "And in his right hand . . ."

"Chips?"

"Exactly."

"You lucked out—I'm me," Kotter said, entering the apartment. "But what if I'd been Mr. Big, but I'd lost all my chips?"

"Mr. Big is a professional gambler, a winner," she told him. "If he'd lost all his chips, he'd be you."

Kotter dropped into a chair and sighed exhaustedly. "I looked everywhere," he said. "No sweathogs."

"Hadn't anyone even seen them?"

Kotter shook his head. "I would have had a lot more success if I'd been looking for six guys in blue serge suits," he said. "They've been everywhere—the pool hall, the printer, McNary's pharmacy, the subway . . ."

"Mr. Big has them!" Julie said tragically.

"That's what I'm afraid of."

There was a knock at the window.

"It's them!" Julie said.

The sweathogs were standing on the fire escape, gesturing wildly. Kotter got up quickly and opened the window. The sweathogs crowded through the opening. They were accompanied by a middle-aged man who bore a striking resemblance to Washington.

"Where have you been?" Kotter demanded. He pointed to the man. "And who's he?"

The man smiled amiably. "Hugo Jonas, sir," he said.

Kotter backed away. "Mr. Big!"

"He's my uncle, Mr. Kotter," Washington said.

Kotter stared at him. "The Mr. Big of international crime is your uncle?" His expression became doubtful. "With a contact like that, how come you're not a big-time criminal?"

"Gabe, it's not always *who* you know that counts," Julie said, defending Washington. "I'm sure aptitude is important, too, even in international crime." She addressed Hugo Jonas. "Isn't that true, Mr. Big?"

"I don't know, lady," he replied. "The closest I ever get to international crime is if I pick up their sanitation."

"He drives a truck for the Sanitation Department," Barbarino told Kotter and Julie.

"Driver of the year," Hugo Jonas said proudly.

"But . . ." Kotter began.

"We had this great story about the Mr. Big of international crime," Washington explained, "only we didn't have a name to go with it. Everybody wanted names. You wanted names, Mr. Kotter. The readers wanted names. So, we got a name."

"My name," Hugo Jonas said. "I lent them the borrow of it."

"For a price," Horshack said.

"Next issue," Washington said, "we're gonna run a big story about Uncle Hugo getting the driver-of-the-year award."

"With pictures," Hugo Jonas said. "Me and my truck and a big pile of sanitation."

"You lied to me!" Kotter said to the sweathogs.

"No, we didn't, Mr. Kotter," Barbarino said. "You asked us if Hugo Jonas was real. He's real, isn't he?"

"You told me he was on a job!"

"He was," Barbarino replied. "He was driving his truck. That's a job. I told you he was cleaning up. That's what he was doing."

Kotter sat down again. He shook his head, trying to clear his thoughts.

"How did we know the FBI would come after us?"

Washington said. "What are they fooling around with us for?"

"They don't want you, they want Mr. Big," Kotter told him.

"Why me?" Hugo Jonas said. "Why don't they get after those litterers?"

"Where have you been?" Kotter asked the sweathogs. "I looked everywhere for you."

"We were hiding out in the back of Uncle Hugo's truck," Washington said.

"With the sanitation," Horshack said. "It was very interesting. Do you realize that there is a great similarity between sanitation and garbage?"

"It's not the same at all," Hugo Jonas said. "Garbage is what people throw out. Sanitation is what we pick up."

"What do we do now, Mr. Kotter?" Barbarino asked. "We don't want to hide out the rest of our lives."

"Not unless the people in this neighborhood clean up their sanitation a little," Horshack said. "It's a disgrace."

"I think we better call in the FBI and tell them that your story was a fraud," Kotter said. "When they find out that Hugo Jonas is not the Mr. Big of international crime, that will be the end of it."

"What if they don't believe us?" Epstein asked.

"Why wouldn't they believe you? You have the proof. You have Hugo Jonas." He turned to Washington's uncle. "Can you prove that you work for the Department of Sanitation?" he asked. "Do you have some kind of identification?"

"I got my truck parked outside."

"That should be enough." Kotter rose. "I'll call the FBI," he said.

"Tell them the windows need doing again," Julie said.

As Kotter started to pick up the phone, the apartment door flew open. Smith and the five other Smiths burst into the room.

"Do you have my mind bugged?" Kotter asked them.

"Nobody move!" Smith commanded. "This is your FBI!"

"Anybody can dress up in a blue serge suit," Washington said. "Let's see some identification."

Smith pulled out his wallet and flipped it open.

"You're not FBI, you're Diners' Club," Washington said.

"Darn—that always happens!" Smith said, chagrined. "But I've got my identification here somewhere." He began flipping through the card-holders. "Master Charge ... BankAmerica card ... library card ... Social Security card ... American Express ... phony foreign correspondent credentials ..."

"Want to borrow my identification?" one of the other Smiths asked.

"No, no, I've got it here," Smith said, continuing to flip the card-holders. "Phony State Department credentials ... phony cab driver's license ... phony window washers union card ... phony Rolling Stones fan club membership ... Ah—here it is!" He showed his identification to Washington.

"Looks phony to me," Washington said.

"Honest, it's the real thing," Smith said. He indicated the other Smiths. "These guys can vouch for me."

"He's him," the second Smith said.

"Could you do a window?" Julie said to the first Smith. "I think that would settle it. I remember last time how whenever you happened to look down you turned pale."

"That won't be necessary," Kotter said. "Let's get this over with."

"Is that a confession?" Smith asked.

"I don't have anything to confess," Kotter replied. He pointed to the sweathogs. "But they do."

"It's like this," Washington said, addressing the FBI men. "I wrote this story for the school paper, the *Booster*, see? It was a great story about how cool I am. Only we got this assistant principal at school, this Mr. Woodman, and he wouldn't put the story in the school paper. Man . . ."

Kotter interrupted. "Just tell them about the Mr. Big story," he said to Washington.

"Yes, where is this Hugo Jonas?" Smith asked.

Washington pointed to his uncle. "He's right there. So, when Mr. Woodman wouldn't put my story in the school paper," he went on, "we figured what we had to do . . ."

The FBI men were no longer listening. They had surrounded Washington's uncle.

"At last, we meet!" Smith said to Hugo Jonas. "We've tracked you from continent to continent, from metropolis to metropolis, and always you've stayed one step ahead of us!"

"You been looking in the wrong places," Washington's uncle told him. "You should have asked for me down at the Department of Sanitation."

"Listen, don't you want to hear my confession?" Washington complained. "I'm just getting to the best part—where I get the idea for a paper of our own, the *Sweathog*, to put the *Booster* out of business."

The FBI men ignored him.

"Where is the loot from the London bank job?" Smith asked Hugo Jonas.

"I don't know anything about it," he replied. "But if it's on my truck, you're welcome to look through it. It's parked outside."

Smith turned to another Smith. "Check it out!" he barked.

"Into the old computer?" the other Smith asked.

"How else?"

"Well, I haven't had a chance to use my Sherlock Holmes fingerprint outfit in a long time, and I was thinking . . ."

"We're not looking for fingerprints, we're after loot!"

"All right," the other Smith said resignedly, departing. "But I wish we wouldn't depend on that computer so much. I'm getting such a feeling of inadequacy." The apartment door closed behind him.

"This is ridiculous," Kotter said to Smith. "Let the sweathogs explain. Hugo Jonas is not the Mr. Big of international crime. He's Washington's uncle. He's a driver for the Department of Sanitation."

"Driver-of-the-year," Hugo Jonas said.

"Are you still contending that they made up that story in the paper?" Smith asked Kotter.

"Yes. They did." He addressed the sweathogs. "Tell him."

"We did," Barbarino said.

"How do you explain the facts?" Smith asked. "You had dates, times, details."

"We got all that stuff out of some old newspapers," Washington explained. "You go to the library, see, and they got all these old newspapers on microfilm. We looked up the stuff on international crime and put it in our story. *That*'s where we got the dates and times and details."

"And I lent them the borrow of my name," Hugo Jonas said.

"We needed a name—any name," Washington said. "Without names, we couldn't even give the *Sweathog* away."

"See how simple it is?" Kotter said to Smith.

"Simple? It's ingenious!" Smith replied. "It's the most true-sounding phony confession I've ever heard in all my years with the Bureau." He smiled smugly. "But we'll break it." He began removing his jacket. "It's just a matter of time," he said. "Eventually, under intense interrogation, the bad guys always crack." He indicated a chair. "You first," he said to Hugo Jonas.

"I better check on my sanitation," Jonas said, heading for the door. "I had it all separated. That guy could get it mixed up putting it through a computer."

"Mixed up is right," Kotter said. "Your sanitation could start getting bills from a department store in Cincinnati."

One of the Smiths stepped in front of the apartment door.

"But there's no hurry," Jonas said, turning back.

"One thing about sanitation, it can't spoil much more than it is." He sat down in the chair.

Smith began circling the chair, eyeing Hugo Jonas ominously. Jonas, hypnotized by the continuing round-and-round motion, began to nod. His eyelids slowly closed.

Suddenly, Smith halted and shot a question at Jonas. "A fake Van Gogh! A picture titled 'Dr. Gachet.' Painting of a man seated at a table, leaning on his arm. What do you know about it?"

Jonas started, awakened from the nap. "People throw out a lot of pictures," he answered. "It's all sanitation to me." He addressed the others. "Right after a funeral, people toss out of lot of pictures," he said. "We can always tell who died just by going through the sanitation."

"This fake Van Gogh was an almost perfect copy!" Smith snapped. "You made just one mistake, Mr. Big! Your artist neglected to put the table in the painting. Dr. Gachet was leaning on thin air!"

"Before," Barbarino pointed out, "you said he was leaning on his arm."

Smith interrupted the interrogation. "Yes, you see, but in the original the arm is resting on a table," he explained.

"Maybe it was a fold-up table," Epstein said. "Somebody could have taken it away."

"What you're looking for is a table thief," Washington told Smith.

"Not me," Hugo Jonas said. "Anything anybody throws out, it's fair game. If we get it, that makes it sanitation. I don't know how that table got there, but if we picked it up, it wasn't stealing. It just looked like some old table that somebody threw out to us. We're not judges and jury, you know. All we do is enforce the sanitation."

Smith was beginning to perspire. "This is not a real table," he said. "It's a table in a painting."

"Oh!" Washington said. "Somebody ripped-off a painting!"

"The painting is a forgery," Smith said. "It wasn't stolen. We have it in Washington."

"Did you get it off my truck?" Jonas asked. "That's stealing, man. Anything on that truck is sanitation, and it's the property of the City of New York." He looked at Smith narrowly. "You are in trouble!"

Smith pulled out a handkerchief and wiped perspiration from his brow. "I'll get back to you later," he said to Hugo Jonas. He turned to Horshack. "Sit down!"

Horshack dropped into a chair. There was a crackling sound.

"You're cracking already!" Smith said, encouraged.

Horshack reached into his pocket and pulled out a handful of broken egg shells. "I think these are the property of the City of New York," he said, handing them to Hugo Jonas.

Smith sagged. "I knew it was too soon."

"You can't just hand this stuff back to me like that," Jonas told Horshack. "This is lost or stolen property that's been returned. You got to come down to the Department of Sanitation and fill out some forms." He passed the egg shells back to Horshack. "Till then, they're in your possession."

"What kind of forms?" Horshack asked.

"Lost or stolen property forms. And if anything happens to them egg shells in the meantime, *you* are responsible."

"Forget the egg shells!" Smith roared. He dabbed nervously at his forehead with the handkerchief. "How does Mr. Big transport pot from one continent to another?" he demanded, directing the question at Horshack.

But it was Washington who answered. "He just flaps his arms and flies, man ... fliiiiies ..." he said dreamily.

"That reminds me of the old days," Hugo Jonas said. "Now, you don't see much of them. But, back then, they were all over the sanitation and all over the truck and all over us."

"What?" Smith asked.

"Flies," Jonas replied. "Horseflies. Did you ever see a horsefly?"

"Man-o-War was pretty fast," Kotter said.

"Stop!" Smith raged. "I see what you're doing! You're leading me on a wild goose chase!"

"That's an oldie, too," Kotter said. "Why did the wild goose cross the road?"

Jonas chuckled. "He was after some chicken," he said.

"I'm taking you all in!" Smith announced.

"In where?" Washington asked.

"Headquarters! We'll continue the interrogation there!"

"May I make a phone call?" Kotter asked.

"Of course. A lawyer is not necessary, however. You're not under arrest. You're merely in custody."

"I'm not going to call a lawyer," Kotter said, going to the phone, "I'm going to call the newspapers."

Smith winced.

"I think they'll be interested," Kotter said. "It isn't every day that an employee of the Sanitation Department—driver-of-the-year, no less—is accused of being the Mr. Big of international crime."

"You're bluffing!" Smith said.

Kotter picked up the receiver.

At the same moment, the apartment door opened. A stranger was standing there. He had an extremely large nose, which appeared to be held on with a rubber band, and stiff, bright red hair, which stuck out at all angles from under his beanie, and he was wearing a blue serge suit.

Kotter put the receiver down.

"Smith—is that you?" Smith asked.

"I'm trying out my Sherlock Holmes disguise kit," the other Smith replied, entering. "How did you know it was me?"

"You *always* need a haircut!" Smith told him. "What did the computer tell you?"

"The same thing it always says—puckita-puckita-puckita."

"I'm talking about the read-out!" Smith said. "What was the read-out?"

"Well, you know what they say about computers: garbage in; garbage out."

Hugo Jonas corrected him. "That's 'sanitation in; sanitation out.' "

"You mean?" Smith said to the other Smith.

The other Smith nodded. "According to the computer, that truck was full of garbage."

"Sanitation," Jonas said.

"No loot?" Smith asked, shaken. "Not even a *little* loot?"

"Well ... there was a folding table in there," the other Smith told him. "But I pulled it out before it went through the computer. It will look nice in my den at home."

"No, you don't!" Jonas said. "That's lost or stolen property. You got forms to fill out, Buster!"

Kotter picked up the receiver again.

"No, wait!" Smith said. "It may not be necessary for us to take *all* of you in, after all. We can't go back to headquarters empty-handed, of course. But perhaps one of you will be enough." He pointed at Horshack. "That one."

"He don't go nowhere with those eggshells," Hugo Jonas told Smith. "That's City of New York property and he's responsible. The only place he goes is down to the Department of Sanitation."

"Oh, all right," Smith said testily. He suddenly brightened. "We'll accept a volunteer!" he said. "Who's for headquarters?"

There was no response.

"How about you, stranger—you with the red hair?" Smith said to the other Smith.

The other Smith shook his head. "I kind of like it here," he said. "These are the kind of people, I bet, who'd let me play with my fingerprint outfit."

"You're the volunteer!" Smith snapped. "That's an order!"

"Shucks!"

"All right, we have our man," Smith told Kotter. "We'll take him in and interrogate him. But don't think this lets the rest of you off the hook. This case is still under investigation." He looked steely-eyed at Hugo Jonas. "I know a Mr. Big of international crime when I see him, not matter what his cover," he said. He strode toward the door. "Bring the suspect!" he barked to the Smiths who were not the other Smith.

They grabbed the other Smith and, following Smith, hustled him from the apartment.

For a second, there was quiet.

Then Julie suddenly ran from the apartment, trailing the FBI men, crying, "Wait! Wait!"

"Looks like you lost your wife," Hugo Jonas said to Kotter. "Happens all the time. It's the uniform that gets them."

"I'm sure it's not that," Kotter said.

"Oh, yes. I know. When I'm wearing my uniform, the girlies are all over me like flies." He looked thoughtful for a moment. "Or maybe those are flies."

"No, I meant I'm sure I haven't lost my wife," Kotter said.

A moment later, Julie returned, looking disgruntled.

"What was that all about?" Kotter asked her.

"I tried to get them to come back and do the windows again next week," she explained.

"They wouldn't?"

She shook her head. "They'll be too busy fighting the never-ending battle for truth, justice and the American way, they told me."

Hugo Jonas snorted derisively. "Big talk!" he said. "I'll bet we'll never see that folding table again. But," he said, turning to Horshack, "we saved the egg shells. Come along, youngster. You've got forms to fill out."

"We'll go along," Washington said, motioning to the other sweathogs.

"How many forms?" Horshack asked Jonas glumly.

"Oh, fifty, sixty."

"What do they do with all those forms?" Horshack asked, appalled.

"Throw them out," Jonas replied, leading the way to the door. "Anything that adds to the sanitation is good for the department." He put a fatherly arm around Horshack's shoulders as they and the other sweathogs departed. "It'll be a job filling out those forms," he said, "but, don't forget, after six months, if nobody has claimed them, those egg shells will be all yours."

"Gee," Horshack said, "I've never had my own egg shells. I come from a big family. I always get hand-me-downs."

"That's how it was for me when I was a kid," Jonas told him. "In a way, it's how it *still* is."

The door closed.

"What did he mean by that?" Julie asked Kotter.

"He rarely sees anything brand-new. When it gets to the garbage can, it's been used."

"That's sad," Julie said. "I wish we had something new to throw out for sanitation," she said, looking around the apartment.

"We do have something new."

"What?"

"Listen!" Kotter said. "The peace! The quiet!"

Julie listened. She began to smile contentedly. "On second thought—let's keep it."

TEN

When classes convened the next morning, Washington and Epstein were not in their seats.

"Anybody know where they are?" Kotter asked.

Barbarino looked carefully into the two empty seats. "They're not here," he reported.

"This class had done you a lot of good," Kotter told him. "When you first came to me, I don't think you could have figured that out." He addressed Horshack. "Do *you* know where they are?"

"Two choices," Horshack replied. "Late or absent. Hahh . . . hahh . . . hahh . . . hahh . . ."

"I hope they're not out on another big story," Kotter said. "You're supposed to work on the *Sweathog* on your own time, not school time."

"They're not on a story," Barbarino said. "The Mr. Big story was enough to last us for a long time. I'm not even going to read anybody else's newspaper any more until they stop filling them with all those stories."

"Do I detect some bitterness?" Kotter said.

"We figured up how much money we made after Happy Harrison took out all his halves," Horshack said. "Not counting the dime Washington cheated himself out of once when he was making change, we broke even."

"That's not much for all those weeks of work," Kotter said.

"Right. Divide it by all the weeks and we probably made even less than even."

"I'm sure it wasn't a total loss, though," Kotter said.

"I got my poem in the paper," Rosalie said. "That's *something.*"

"We all got our names in the paper," Epstein added. "That's something too. Not much, though, since it was our own paper."

"But you learned a lot, I'm sure," Kotter said. "You added to your store of knowledge."

"Then why do I feel that in the store of newspapering knowledge my shelves are empty?" Horshack asked. "Hahh . . . hahh . . . hahh . . . hahh . . ."

"Perhaps . . ." Kotter began.

He was interrupted by the arrival of Washington and Epstein.

"Do you have 'late' slips?" Kotter asked.

"After last night, helping Horshack fill out all those forms," Washington replied, "we decided to cut through the red tape. No more 'late' slips."

"Your Uncle Hugo won't be very happy about that," Kotter said.

"Why not?"

"Because, after you give me the 'late' slips, I throw them away. They add to the sanitation. Anything that adds to the sanitation is good for Uncle Hugo—the former Mr. Big."

"We'll make up for it, Mr. Kotter," Horshack said. "We'll donate those files in the corner of your apartment to sanitation."

Kotter addressed Washington again. "May I ask, then, why you're late?"

"I had to meet a guy in an alley," he replied.

"A fight?"

"Nah, that coach from that private school. I told him it's no deal. We can't give him that publicity in the *Sweathog*."

"You're passing up that opportunity—the scholarship, the grades?" Kotter said, pleased.

Washington shrugged indifferently. "Yeah."

"I stopped at McNary's Pharmacy, Mr. Kotter," Epstein said. "I told him we're not going to run that story, that put-down on Finnery's Pharmacy."

"What did he say to that?"

"He cancelled all his ads."

"How did the coach react?" Kotter asked Washington.

"Like a man," Washington replied. "He beat his head against the wall."

"I'm proud of you . . . proud of both of you," Kotter said to Washington and Epstein. "You met bribery eyeball to eyeball and bribery flinched."

"It wasn't so hard," Washington said. "There isn't going to be any *Sweathog* any more."

"You're folding the paper?"

"No, we're gonna *stop* folding it, we're giving it up."

Kotter smiled. "Things won't be the same at the apartment," he said.

"You know, that office ..." Washington said. "Since we won't be needing it any more, maybe we could rent it out to somebody else."

"It's no longer there," Kotter told him. "I used my magic kit and turned it back into a living room. Is that unanimous?" he asked, speaking to the other sweathogs. "The paper is dead?"

The response was a chorus of sounds that confirmed the passing.

"But you wanted to close down the *Booster*," Kotter said. "What about that?"

"I guess it just doesn't make any difference," Washington replied. "It's not like the *Booster* is something bad that's hurting somebody. It's nothing, man. Nobody pays any attention to it."

"Yeah, if the *Booster* lives or dies, it will make about as much difference as whether there's ever another Miss America or not," Barbarino said. "Besides Bert Parks, who cares?"

The door opened and Mr. Woodman entered.

"I'm sure I'm not interrupting anything important," Woodman said to Kotter. "Not in *this* class."

"No, we've dropped our paper clip straightening project," Kotter answered.

"I have been in communication with the government," Woodman announced.

"Flunked your tax audit, eh?" Kotter said.

"I am referring to the FBI. They have informed me that the Mr. Big investigation has been temporarily suspended permanently."

"That ought to slow it down, at least," Kotter said.

"Kotter, this is serious business," Woodman said.

"Those brave men are fighting the never-ending battle for truth, justice and the American way."

"You might have trouble remembering that, too, if you'd seen the guy in the red fright wig and the false nose," Kotter said.

"I don't know what you're talking about." He sighed. "But, then, I seldom do." He faced the sweathogs. "There is another serious matter," he said. "That newspaper, the *Sweathog*."

"Mr. Woodman, we . . ." Washington began.

Woodman interrupted. "I know," he said huffily, "you think you have me right where you want me. You think *you* can call the tune and I'll have to dance to it. Well, you're wrong."

"Mr. Woodman . . ." Washington tried again.

"No, I'm doing the talking," Woodman said.

Washington shrugged and sat back.

"I asked you nicely to stop publishing the *Sweathog*," Woodman went on.

"When was that?" Kotter asked.

"When I called in the lawyer," Woodman replied. "If I'd used my authority, I would have *ordered* them to shut down that paper. But, no, to spare their feelings, I tried to get the lawyer to order them to do it."

"But now, no more Mr. Nice Guy?" Kotter guessed.

"You're exactly right." He faced the sweathogs once more. "I *demand* that you put an end to that paper!"

The only response from the sweathogs, who had already decided to stop publishing the paper, anyway, was a yawn from Washington.

"That attitude will get you nowhere!" Woodman

told them. "When I issue an order, I expect it to be obeyed, or . . ."

"Heads will roll," Kotter said.

Horshack, who had been up late the night before filling out forms, slid down in his seat and closed his eyes.

"I get the impression that you're not impressing them," Kotter said to Woodman. "I wonder if it's because that lawyer told you to keep hands off the *Sweathog* or end up on Staten Island—which is hard by the great state of New Jersey."

"Well . . . maybe I could rephrase my demand . . ." Woodman said.

"Yes, you could beg," Kotter said. "But, frankly, do you really think it would do any good? The *Sweathog* is a huge success. What could you possibly say that would persuade the sweathogs to give that up?"

"Nothing . . ." Woodman replied feebly.

"Still . . . there might be a way," Kotter said. "Out of the goodness of their hearts, the sweathogs might be willing to make a trade."

"Oh, yeah," Washington said.

Woodman looked at Kotter warily. "Trade . . . ?"

"Let's go back to the beginning," Kotter said. "Remember why the sweathogs started their paper?"

"Pure rowdyism!" Woodman said.

"No. As an alternative to the *Booster*. If there was a change in the *Booster*, though, there would be no more need for the *Sweathog*."

"How *much* change?" Woodman asked.

"Dump it, man," Washington said.

"I don't think it would be necessary to go that far," Kotter said. "I think it would help, though," he told

Woodman, "if you turned the *Booster* over to the students."

"Never!" Woodman responded.

"Long live the *Sweathog!*" Barbarino said.

"Well, maybe 'never' is a little too strong," Woodman said. "What I could do is name a committee to study the situation. And, in a few years . . ."

"We got to turn our reporters loose on that paper clip story again," Washington said to Barbarino. "That's what our readers want—local scandal."

"Wrong-doing in high places—local," Barbarino agreed.

"Actually," Woodman said, "I've been spending too much time on the *Booster*, anyway. I have much more important things to do."

"Yeah, you got to make those citizens arrests for running in the halls," Epstein said. "You're probably behind on your quota."

"It's about time the students took the responsibility for the school paper," Woodman said testily. "They can't expect me to do *everything* for them."

"Set 'em straight, man!" Washington said. "Lower the boom!"

"I intend to do exactly that!" Woodman said. "I'll tell the student editors today! From now on, they're on their own! I've coddled them long enough!"

"In that case, I see no more need for the *Sweathog*," Kotter said. "Of course, that isn't *my* decision to make."

"If the students are going to take over the *Booster*," Washington said, "we'd be smart to go out of business with the *Sweathog*."

"That's a smart move you made, Mr. Woodman," Horshack said. "You beat us."

"The outcome was never in doubt," Woodman replied. "I've had a lot more experience than you have in this dog-eat-dog world."

"I'll bet you polish off a St. Bernard and a couple Chihuahuas before you even start breakfast," Kotter said admiringly.

"Symbolically speaking, that's not far from the truth," Woodman replied. He faced the class again. "I hope you've learned something from this," he said. "Never tangle with the Old Man!"

Washington addressed Kotter. "He's pushing it, man," he said. "In a minute, he's gonna have us back in the newspaper business."

"I'm leaving!" Woodman said quickly, hurrying toward the door. "Things to do—important things!"

"The paper clips are really gonna get it!" Washington said, as Woodman disappeared through the doorway.

"Congratulations," Kotter said to the sweathogs. "Your paper accomplished a real public service."

"I'll miss it," Barbarino said.

"Why did you give it up, then?" Kotter said.

"I won't miss the paper," Barbarino said. "I'll miss all that food we got at your place."

"To be completely honest," Kotter said, "I'll miss having the newspaper office in the apartment too. No more slamming doors. The telephone won't be ringing every two minutes. No more arguments about which story goes where."

"You'll miss that?" Horshack said.

"Yes." Kotter smiled euphorically. "And it feels so *good!*"